P.

"I'm not self-destruc

"Whatever the hell label you'd like to put on it, this mountainside isn't safe in a storm."

Lightning cracked and thunder boomed.

"That's it," she said. "Finish this mission—or death wish—on your own." She took Sallie from him, tucking her into the stroller, then fastening her safety harness. "We'll hopefully see you back at the house."

She'd already gone a good fifty feet down the trail when he called, "Camille, hold up!"

"Why?"

"Because you're right."

Lightning again cracked.

Hands on his hips, he looked to the sky. "I thought if I climbed high enough, far enough, I could escape this pain. Why do people I love keep dying? Em and Chase. Both of our dads. Your grandmother. So many of my SEAL brothers. Sometimes it feels like I'm the last man standing."

"But you're not..." Her voice was soft enough to barely reach him. "You have me." *At least for a little while.*

"But I don't deserve you—never did."

Dear Reader,

When hubby and I left the hospital with our newborn twins, we turned down my mom and grandmother's offer to help. Why? I'd spent months devouring parenting books and knew this was the proper time to "bond." Ha!

We'd been home maybe thirty minutes when both babies began *screaming*. We couldn't figure out how to work the bottle liners or the fancy cloth diapers we'd been given as a shower gift. It was complete bedlam. I got on the phone and called in all the help we could get!

While writing Jed and Camille's story, memories flooded back of those first few months we never thought we'd live through. Looking back, those were some of the most hectic, but happiest times of my life. Late-night feedings were the best. Hubby and I would each take a baby, then watch MTV. (That was back when they played actual music videos! LOL!)

I can't imagine raising triplets under such tragic circumstances, but Jed and Camille pull together to become surprisingly great parents—at least until stress tears them apart. Will they find love? You'll have to keep turning pages to find out...

Happy reading!

Laura Marie xoxo

HOME *on the* RANCH
THE COLORADO COWBOY'S TRIPLETS

———— ⚒ ————

LAURA MARIE ALTOM

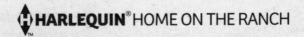

HARLEQUIN® HOME ON THE RANCH

Recycling programs
for this product may
not exist in your area.

ISBN-13: 978-1-335-54298-4
ISBN-13: 978-1-335-63397-2 (Direct to Consumer edition)

Home on the Ranch: The Colorado Cowboy's Triplets

Printed in U.S.A.

Laura Marie Altom is a bestselling and award-winning author who has penned nearly fifty books. After college—go, Hogs!—Laura Marie did a brief stint as an interior designer before becoming a stay-at-home mom to boy-girl twins and a bonus son. Always an avid romance reader, she knew it was time to try her hand at writing when she found herself replotting the afternoon soaps.

When not immersed in her next story, Laura plays video games, tackles Mount Laundry and, of course, reads romance!

Laura loves hearing from readers either at PO Box 2074, Tulsa, OK 74101, or by email, balipalm@aol.com.

Love winning fun stuff? Check out lauramariealtom.com.

Books by Laura Marie Altom

Home on the Ranch: Colorado Cowboy SEAL

Harlequin Western Romance

Cowboy SEALs

The SEAL's Miracle Baby
The Baby and the Cowboy SEAL
The SEAL's Second Chance Baby
The Cowboy SEAL's Jingle Bell Baby
The Cowboy SEAL's Christmas Baby
Cowboy SEAL Daddy

Visit the Author Profile page at Harlequin.com for more titles.

For Grandma Lu and Grandpa Joe.
I love you beyond words.

he stupid out of their unmentionables. "But your

going apeshit in your office."

D Bartoni growled. "I've got my eye on you, Mon-

Yessir." Jed dropped onto his belly in preparation
his next rounds.

He was good to go until overhearing snippets of
heated conversation taking place in the CO's field
ffice—an ammo box he used for a seat in the shade
f their transport vehicle.

"…tell him. You're his closest friend."

Adam said, "But he's in a good place, sir."

"Fine." The CO stood. "I'll deliver the news."

"No. Let me." Ad

"**M**onroe, you hit worse than a pack of third-grade
girls in a tickle fight!"

"Yessir." Even though Navy SEAL Jed Monroe
had sunk four of his last five shots into the long-range
shooting target's bull's-eye, he saluted his CO and
sucked up the constructive criticism like a man—like
a freakin' SEAL. God, he loved his job. Was there any
more beautiful place in the world than the Naval Am-
phibious Base in Coronado, California? Toss in this
sunny May day and having his life finally back on
track and he reckoned it would be impossible to top this
level of contentment. "I'll nail them all next time, sir."

"You'd damn well better, or I'll demote your sorry—"

"Excuse me, Chief!" Fellow SEAL Adam Rhodes
cleaned sand from his weapon. The rest of the sixteen-
man platoon had been sent on an open-ocean swim to

Chapter 1

...Adam's expression was g...
headed Jed's way.

Jed raised his hand to his forehead, shading his eyes from the already hot morning sun. *What the hell's going on?*

His stomach turned queasy.

So much for his great mood...

When Adam's shadow blocked the sun, Jed rolled onto his back and groaned. "If this is about Alyssa, who has a nasty habit of popping in and out of my life, just keep on walking. Now that she and Mr. Hollywood are officially hitched, she's not my problem." Only she was, because he still couldn't believe that after two happy— okay, *mostly* happy—years of marriage, she'd cheated on him and was now married to another guy.

"Sorry, man." Adam bowed his head. "Shit. I don't even know how to say this..."

"Spit it out. Did something happen to my mom?" She worked as a traveling nurse at missionaries and remote villages in parts of Africa that were notoriously dangerous. He prayed every night she'd live to see the next day. For years, he'd begged her to head back to the States, find a nice condo and spend her golden years reading on some nice beach.

"No."

"My sister or the babies?" Emily just had triplets and could be the official spokesperson for Fairy Tales-R-Us. She and her husband, Chase, weren't just blissfully happy, but rainbows and unicorns happy. For real. During the heat of his divorce, watching the two of them together had hurt. Now that they had the triplets, whereas most sane people would go off the deep end, Emily and Chase's world had only grown brighter. "I keep telling her to move closer to town. I know Chase fancies himself a cattle rancher, but those babies are tiny—only ten weeks old. They get sick and it's like a good hour to the nearest clinic—all the way to Aspen for a legit hospital." He knew he was rambling, but couldn't seem to stop. "Emily is constantly lecturing me on being more positive, but I'm all about keeping it real."

Adam rubbed his closed eyes with his thumb and forefinger.

"If Mom, Emily and the babies are good, then what's the problem?" His physician father had passed from an aneurysm ten years earlier. The ladies in his life were all the family Jed had—aside from Chase. Wait… "Is it my brother-in-law? Is he hurt?"

"Shit…" Adam kicked at the sand. "There's no good way to say this. Chase is dead. Freak heart attack."

"Wait—*what?*" Jed wasn't sure if it was the heat or the news, but his mind was spinning. He stood, only to stumble, grabbing hold of the transport vehicle's side mirror to keep his wobbly legs upright. "Has to be a mistake."

He gazed out at the calm Pacific, where the rest of his team finished their swim.

The sun shone just as brightly.

The surf's steady crash sounded just as relaxing.

Yet in that instant, his entire world had changed.

"Somehow your mom got ahold of the CO's wife. Your sister's inconsolable and there's no way your mom can return to the States anytime soon. Emily needs you in Colorado ASAP."

"Take the truck back to base." In a rare show of compassion, the CO cupped his hand to Jed's shoulder. "I'll radio for another. Go to your sister. The few times I met her, she seemed like a nice gal. I'll file the necessary paperwork for your leave. Take as long as you need."

"Yessir." Numb, Jed knew he should be running toward the truck. Toward his little sis. But he couldn't move. All he could do was stare out at his SEAL brothers, the weight of the news he'd just received anchoring him in place.

"Change in plans." Hands on his hips, the CO turned to Adam. "Monroe's in no shape to drive. You take him and help find the necessary flights."

"Yessir." Adam saluted their CO before turning to his friend.

"I've got this." Jed brushed off Adam's help, then struggled to his feet. "I'm good. Just needed a minute. This is a lot to take in, but Emily's strong. I'm sure I'll be back in a few days…"

"Jed?"

"Camille?"

The mere sight of her former fiancé gave retired Miami detective Camille Hall cold-hot chills.

The last time they'd been together...

The hurtful things they'd both said...

The love she'd felt for him that had been too intense—like standing too close to fire. Her soul had instinctively known surrendering her heart to him would only get her burned.

Hugging herself, she stepped back from Grandpa Ollie's Colorado cabin door. Past nine on a cold and windy Thursday night, there were zero logical reasons for the only man she'd ever loved to be standing in the dim porch light, piercing green eyes red-rimmed from...*tears?*

Jed didn't cry.

As far as she'd known, he had *never* cried—certainly not when their relationship had been decimated as effectively as if there were such a thing as a heart grenade.

"What's wrong?" *Why are you here?* She willed her runaway pulse to slow. "Are Em and the babies okay?"

He nodded, then shook his head.

"I owe her and Chase a visit, but I've only been back in town a few days," she said. Part of the reason she hadn't visited her longtime friend was because of how much Emily and Chase's home—the family home where she'd spent so much time during endless summers with Emily and Jed—reminded her of him and the happy times they'd shared.

"You don't know?"

"Know what?" Her heart had been pounding, but now stopped.

From deeper inside the house blared gunshots from one of her grandfather's favorite Westerns. A cowboy shouted, "That's right! Run, you lily-livered toad sucker!"

"Tell me. What's wrong?" When Jed's expression paled to the point she feared he might puke in the bushes, she left the house to put her arm around him. Though touching him should have felt achingly familiar, her motions were stiff. More of an autopilot reflex courtesy than a case of *wanting* her arms around him.

But to be fair, their breakup was very much two-sided.

"Chase is dead." After a sharp exhale, he brushed his hand over his military-buzzed hair. "Em is on her way to the hospital in Aspen. I think she may have accidentally overdosed."

"*What?* I just saw Chase a few months ago. He was fine."

"Sudden heart attack. Total fluke."

"*Ohmygosh.*" She covered her mouth with trembling hands. As if hit by a physical blow, she grasped a porch post.

"Anyway, I was going to ask Ollie to watch the girls while I go to Em."

"Gramps is crashed in his recliner, but I'll do it—as long as you need. Go."

"Thanks." He jerked his thumb toward the SUV. "Mind helping me unload?"

"Right. Of course." There were a hundred questions she wanted to ask, but they could wait. Her lingering personal pain over his quickie marriage meant nothing compared to this current disaster. But now that her heart had mentioned it, where was his wife?

Working in tandem, it took maybe fifteen minutes to haul diaper bags and blankets inside and assemble the portable playpen Jed had thought to bring for use as a crib.

Ollie continued snoring while she and Jed transformed his living room into a temporary nursery.

Camille muted the TV before they brought in the babies.

Jed took two infants from their car safety seats, while Camille took the third into her arms.

"I still can't believe this happened," she said. "Last I saw him, Chase was barbecuing chicken on their deck while it snowed." She and Emily had watched, laughing while gumball-sized flakes messed with his saucing technique.

"Em's gutted. I've never seen her like this. Not even when our dad died."

"Go to her. I'm happy to keep the girls as long as you need."

"Thanks." He hovered near the door. "I put extra formula in one of the diaper bags."

"No worries. Gramps has a spare key to Emily and Chase's house. If I run out of essentials, it's a quick trip over."

The set of his mouth grim, he nodded. "Again, thanks for helping on such short notice. Hopefully I won't be long and will bring my sister home in the morning."

"I'll say a prayer for her. Drive careful. That road's a beast at night."

"Will do."

He slipped out of the suddenly too warm house and into the dark. Camille stood at the door, watching him go. Between them, they'd said goodbye to far too many people. Her grandmother and father. His father and now brother-in-law.

Each other.

As his taillights faded into the dirt road's rising

dust, she pressed her hands to her chest. "Please God, let Emily be all right. Please don't let her be the next loss…"

Not hearing any crying or fussing, Camille took her time heading back inside. She breathed in gallons of cool, damp night air. Eyes closed, she whispered a few more fervent prayers.

Then she forced herself back to reality—to the fact that she had suddenly become the temporary caregiver of newborn triplets.

In the cabin, with the front door closed and locked behind her, she found her grandfather not only awake, but cantankerous.

"What's wrong with the TV?" Ollie snatched the remote from the table beside his recliner and gave it a shake. "The sound's not coming out, and this is the best part."

"The TV's quiet because I muted it. Look…" She nodded toward the three wide-eyed infants staring up at the cabin's pine-plank ceiling. "We have company."

"What in the world are Emily and Chase's girls doing here?"

She sat hard on the sofa. "Did you hear Chase died?"

"*What?* That can't be right."

"That's what I said."

"He was so young. Why didn't we hear anything?"

She snorted. "Probably because you're so crotchety no one wants to even stop by for a visit."

He grunted.

Only a few minutes later, he'd drifted back into a deep sleep.

One of the babies fussed.

While Camille technically knew all their names, now

that she was seeing them in a row, she didn't have a clue which name went with which identical cherubic face.

"I should have had your uncle put name tags on you," she said, while scooping the fussy cutie from the playpen. The baby settled her chubby cheek against Camille's breasts and promptly fell asleep.

The feeling of trust placed in her by this tiny, perfect being was indescribable. More than anything, Camille had always wanted to be a mom. Then she'd earned a coveted position on the Miami-Dade County Special Victims Bureau and everything changed.

She'd believed the promotion had been a dream come true—a chance to sink her teeth into meaty cases that truly mattered. What she hadn't expected were daily emotional gut-punches stemming from viewing unfathomably horrific crime scenes or meeting with victims' grief-stricken families. Then there were the times she'd interacted with the men and even women who'd committed the heinous crimes.

Just thinking about the emptiness in their dark gazes left her chilled.

She gave the baby an extra squeeze, kissing the crown of her head. As much as she loved children, she no longer yearned for motherhood. The risk of losing them—potentially losing herself—was far too great. "Let's get you back with your sisters."

After gingerly placing the infant in the crib alongside her snoozing siblings, she covered them all with their fuzzy pink blankets, taking extra care in making sure their tiny toes were protected from the night's chill.

"You're next," she said to her still-sleeping grandfather, giving his shoulder a light shake. "Hey, Gramps. Let's call it a night."

He grunted, slow to wake or even recognize his surroundings. "What?"

"Come on…" She took his hands, planting her feet to help him from his chair. "Let's get you to bed."

"I need to pee."

"For now, let's just get you out of your recliner and down the hall."

"I'm fine." Finally on his feet, he grunted again. "All this coddling is gonna give me heartburn."

"Duly noted." She kept a firm hold on his arm while he shuffled in his worn house shoes she'd bought him for Christmas ten years earlier. Time for a new pair.

"Was I dreaming, or did you tell me that neighbor boy, Chase, died?"

"He did…"

"Damned shame. He was a good kid. The best I've seen around these parts in a good long while."

She nodded. The loss must have been unimaginably tough for Emily. She still barely had a grasp on caring for three newborns. But to now tackle the job solo?

Impossible.

Once Emily left the hospital, Camille would remind her that she had a lifelong friend just down the road who was ready to lend a hand whenever needed.

As for her feelings for Emily's brother?

Camille released a long, slow exhale.

It took thirty minutes to get her grandfather washed and changed into flannel pj's, then tucked into bed, before convincing him to take his blood pressure medication. Of course, he complained during each step, arguing he was fine sleeping in his clothes, but she argued right back that she wasn't fine with him rolling around in the dust and grime he'd picked up that day while working his mine.

Her grandfather had worked the shafts on his mountain claim all her life. To her knowledge, he had yet to find a thing other than dirt, spiders and tons of worthless rocks, but the task kept him busy and the dream of one day hitting the motherlode kept him alive.

"Good night, Gramps," she finally said, with a kiss to his weathered cheek. "Sweet dreams."

He delivered his usual grunt.

Before switching off his bedside lamp, she surveyed his mess of a room. One more thing to add to her growing to-do list. It wasn't that his room was dirty, just cluttered to the point that her long-deceased grandmother's beautiful antiques were no longer visible beneath piles of survey maps, mining magazines, mining equipment and even a collection of vintage gold pans.

Wearing an indulgent grin, she darkened the room and closed the door on her grandfather's snoring.

Back in the living room, she eyed the portable crib and its three tiny occupants. "Now, what am I going to do with you?"

Since they were sleeping, for the moment her only task was to watch them. Make sure they were safe from any number of things that could do them harm. Choking on toys. Suffocating under their blanket. Kidnappings…

Okay—considering their remote location, that last fear was beyond irrational, but back in Miami, she'd seen it all. In one case she was on, a set of newborn twins had never been found. No doubt they'd been taken, then sold on the black market to some whack-job who had more money than sense.

She collapsed onto her grandfather's recliner, but instead of leaning back, she lurched forward, resting her elbows on her knees. Didn't matter that she was tired. Protecting her precious charges was her top priority.

No matter what, she wouldn't let Jed and Emily down.

Like you did so many other families?

Her pulse hammered and her palms sweated.

How many innocent lives had been lost on her watch? How many families had she destroyed by sharing grim news?

It didn't matter how often her supervisor told her she couldn't take the cases personally.

She had.

Every. Single. One.

These lost, stolen, abused or murdered children weren't just nameless, faceless victims to her, but sons and daughters who had been ripped from families.

Forcing herself to do the deep breathing the department shrink had advised, Camille momentarily felt better. But then her cell rang—shattering her nerves all to hell.

She hadn't heard that merry ringtone in what? Nearly ten years? Camille was surprised Jed still had her number.

After a sharp exhale, she answered, "How's Emily?"

"Holding her own."

"Good."

"How are the babies?"

"Sleepy." *Thank goodness.* Just because she'd always wanted her own children didn't mean she knew the first thing about caring for them.

"They're usually okay until around two a.m., then

all hell breaks loose. Grab yourself some shut-eye until then."

"Will do. How long have you been with her? Here— on the mountain?"

"A couple weeks. Since hearing about Chase."

"How'd you get away?" His insane work schedule had been but one of the myriad reasons their relationship had proved impossible.

"Emergency leave. How about you? Your mom told my mom about your promotion. Why aren't you back in Miami?"

"Long story." She wasn't proud that she'd resigned. She was even less proud of being emotionally incapable of handling the job. Her shrink said burnout in that kind of intense work environment was common— certainly nothing to be ashamed of. But Camille still felt as if she'd let down not only her department, but the dozens—if not hundreds—of children still needing her help.

"I've got time," he said. "Only thing to do around here is pace."

"Let's just say the job wasn't what I thought it would be. When I heard Gramps needed help, this seemed like as good a place as any to regroup."

"True. There's no place on earth like our mountain." Emily and Chase's home had once belonged to Jed's grandparents. They'd left it to Jed's parents, who had gifted it to the once happy couple. Camille had visited her grandparents every school holiday. She and Emily had been best friends. When the girls discovered boys, they'd run with a few teen bull riders from town, but one summer Camille had broken her leg riding and Jed had been grounded for nearly starting the barn on fire with bottle rockets. His punishment had been weeks of hard labor. When his parents had run out of chores for him to do, they'd sent him to Ollie and her grandmother, Mable. A misty smile tugged the corners of Camille's lips when her mind's eye caught on the memory of teen Jed mowing and mucking stalls and weed-eating, all while wearing cowboy boots, Wranglers, his favorite beaten brown leather cowboy hat and nothing on his chest save for sweat coating tanned muscle.

"You still there?"

"Yeah." Camille gave herself a mental kick. Thank goodness her trip down memory lane ended before recalling their first kiss. Gifting each other their virginity. Whispering "I love you" beneath the stars. "Sorry. My mind blanked for a sec."

"No worries. I should let you sleep. I just wanted to check in and thank you again."

"Glad I could help."

"You're a good person, Cam—always have been. Guess all this mess with Chase, and now my sister, has me feeling sentimental, but for what it's worth, I'm sorry. You know, about how things went down between us. I never meant for it to turn out that way."

Her heart skipped a beat. "Me, neither."

"Right. Anyway, with luck, see you in the morning with Emily in tow."

"Sounds good."

Camille disconnected the call and wasn't sure what to think. The last thing she'd expected when returning to Marigold to care for her grandfather had been running into Jed. Or learning that Chase had died. Poor Emily.

At least when Camille lost Jed it had been a choice.

Chapter 2

While ER doctors worked on his sister, Jed paced Aspen Valley Hospital's waiting room. The place looked more like a ski resort than a hospital, which he supposed many patients and families found comforting.

At the moment, he doubted anything would make him feel better aside from learning his sister would be okay.

Although that wasn't entirely true. For the brief time he'd spoken with Camille, the tightness in his chest had lessened. The room's dim light seemed brighter. A million years ago, she'd been not just his best friend and lover, but his everything.

Truth be told, maybe he'd never fully gotten over her. Maybe Alyssa had been somewhat justified in cheating on him if he admitted that his heart had never fully been with her. Part of him would always remain with Camille—not that it mattered.

Though it would be nice catching up with her, what they'd shared was beyond ancient history. Their relationship wasn't a dust-covered box he'd shoved to the back of his mental attic, but something he'd long ago abandoned at the side of the curb for weekly trash removal. Their breakup had hurt so badly that he'd needed the memory gone.

The alternative, of ever revisiting that pain, seemed too cruel.

Three cups of tar-like black coffee later, the sun was just rising when a scrub-wearing doctor emerged from behind pass-code-locked doors. He hung his head, raking his hands through longish salt-and-pepper hair.

Jed ditched his latest coffee in a trash can, then strode to meet the man who held Emily's life in his hands.

"How is she?" Jed asked. "When can I take her home?"

The doctor said nothing, seeming to struggle with his words.

"I get it if she needs to stay longer. She's been through a lot. I mean, the stress alone from the sudden loss of a spouse would do most people in. But she's strong."

"Mr. Monroe..."

"I probably need to grab her a change of clothes and toiletries. A neighbor's watching my nieces, so I'll—"

"Mr. Monroe, I don't even begin to know how to say this, but your sister..." His voice cracked. Exhaustion weighted his shoulders and his eyes were red-rimmed from having pulled an all-nighter.

Stood to reason the guy was tired.

Jed was, too.

"Your sister died."

No. The doctor's words didn't compute.

"We pumped her stomach, but the damage was already done. Approximately thirty minutes ago, she went into cardiac arrest. Every effort was made to save her, but sometimes in suicide victims, there's no will to live."

"She didn't commit suicide. The overdose was *accidental.* I told you that when she was admitted."

"Whatever the case, on behalf of the entire ER team, we're sorry for your loss. The hospital chaplain has been called and will help with arrangements."

"Arrangements?" Jed clenched his fists. Things like calling a funeral home? Explaining to his mom that she'd lost not only her son-in-law, but her only daughter? Sure, he'd get right on all that.

He needed to punch a wall. The doctor's placid face. This wasn't happening.

There was no effing way this was happening.

But it was.

"I—I need to see her," Jed said.

"Of course. I'll have nurses clean her up."

"No—I need to see her now. As she is—*was.* Don't even try keeping me away…"

"Sir!" The doctor grasped Jed's shoulders. "I understand you're hurting, but I promise you don't want your final memory of your sister to be unpleasant. Take a seat. I'll have a nurse get you once Emily is in a private room."

Camille woke in her grandfather's recliner, at first unsure where she was. Then the night came rushing back.

Emily having been taken to the hospital.

Jed dropping off the babies.

That unbearably sweet call that had dredged up memories best left alone.

Her throat ached from holding back tears, but with three babies to care for, she didn't have the luxury of breaking down.

She raised her gaze to find the crib empty.

Pulse instantly racing, she rose, convinced that the triplets had not only been taken, but worse. Then she felt like an idiot upon hearing her grandfather singing "The Itsy Bitsy Spider" in the kitchen.

After a quick trip to her room to change into a fresh T-shirt, she ducked into the hall bathroom for her morning routine. Splashing cold water on her face made her feel better, but still tired.

"About time," her grandfather said when she entered the kitchen. He'd shoved the round oak table into a corner, making room for a quilt that the babies lounged on while staring at themselves in the shiny sides of stainless-steel pots and pans. "When you were a little past this age, your favorite thing in the world was playing with kitchen gear. Your grandmother had special cabinets for you that the second she'd set you on the floor, you'd make a beeline for." He smiled and shook his head. "Cute as a button, you were. What happened?"

He busted out laughing.

She landed a mock punch to his shoulder. "Why am I even here?"

"Because you're the person I can always rely on to take the best care of me."

"You're perfectly capable of caring for yourself."

"True." He shrugged. "But it's a heckuva lot more fun with you around. Now, I'd say we've got maybe ten or twenty minutes before all hell breaks loose with these three cabbage patch kiddos. Do you have any idea how to make their formula?"

"No, but at that *fancy place you sent me called college, I learned to read real good.*" She winked. "Just throwing this out there, but maybe we should read the packaging directions?"

He laughed again.

She sent silent thanks to the heavens that she had him in her life. He'd been her one constant, the person she could go to with any problem and he innately knew how to fix it—except for her breakup with Jed. He'd always said they'd one day be together.

Boy, had he been wrong.

"When are you and Jed planning on giving me great-grandbabies?" Gramps asked, midway through the bottle prep process.

"First, there's no such thing as me and Jed. Second, since what I've seen on my job, you know how I feel about bringing more kids into this ugly world."

"My world isn't ugly. Up here, the most serious crime wave I recall is a string of cattle rustlings back in 1986."

"Clearly, you don't read the paper. Have you seen the crime reports in Glenwood Springs or Denver— even Aspen?"

"Nope. Never much saw the need to go borrowing trouble when I don't have any."

"It doesn't hurt to be well-informed of your surroundings."

"Pfft." He waved off her concerns. "Ask me, all you're doing is looking for trouble where there isn't any. According to your mom, besides babysitting me, you came out here to relax. Don't you think it's high time you got started?"

"Thanks, *Judge*. I'll take the matter under advisement."

Working side by side, they made enough formula to fill three bottles, then she parked her grandfather in his recliner to feed a baby in the crook of each arm. He'd probably cramp from holding their bottles, but he deserved it after all the grief he'd given her about Jed and her justified views on crime.

She took the third baby—she'd given up on keeping their names straight—to the rocker where her grandmother had reportedly nursed her mom when she'd been a newborn. Though Camille would never admit it to her grandfather, the connection to her past, to the repressed woman buried inside who would like nothing more than to believe the fairy tale of safe, happy families truly existing, did soothe her aching heart.

Sadly, her brain knew better than to believe everything would be okay.

Case in point, this tragedy with Emily and Chase. Feel-good endings were Hollywood or Hallmark creations. They rarely—if ever—played out in real life. Jed's poor sister was now stuck raising three babies alone, forever dreaming of how things might have been had her husband survived.

Tragic.

Beyond horrible.

Which was why Camille planned to forever protect her heart. If she never let anyone in, she stood a far less chance of getting hurt.

Jed paused in the bustling hospital hall before entering the room where he'd see his dead sister. *Dead*. The word didn't seem real. How was this happening?

One minute he'd been rambling to her about making popcorn, and now…

His throat clogged with unshed emotion. His eyes stung.

The thought occurred to him that maybe he shouldn't do this alone? But while he had friends still in the area, his SEAL brothers were in Coronado.

His mom was unreachable…

Camille.

The knot at the back of his throat tightened.

As much as he'd now appreciate her support, he no longer deserved it. Even if he did, it wasn't as if they were friends. The only reason they'd even spoken was because of the extreme emergency. Once this initial crisis passed, his mom would be with the triplets, and he'd return to his base. And Camille? Well, he wasn't sure what she'd do. The only thing he was sure of was that she wouldn't want anything more to do with him.

Forcing a breath, he pushed open the door to the private room.

Only a dim light shone above the bed and curtains had been drawn on the sunny day. The stench of cleaning chemicals accosted his senses.

From where he stood midway into the private hospital room, Emily could have been sleeping. Some kind soul had brushed her hair and dressed her in a fresh blue gown. The bed linens were drawn high and the scene was as peaceful as he supposed it could be.

But the closer he stepped, the more last night's chaos raged in his head.

"Where you headed?" he asked, when his sister wobbled while rising from the sofa. In the process, she

knocked several prescription bottles to the floor. "Need help?"

After shaking her head, she teetered toward the kitchen. "Wather."

"What?" He trailed her. "Hon, are you okay?"

"I—I'm so sad. I—I took extra and I still cry."

"You're not making sense. How many of your tranquilizers did you take?"

She shook her head. "I love my…s-so much. Why can't better mom?" Tears wetted her cheeks.

"The babies? I love them, too. You're a great mom. But back to your medicine. How much do you think you took?"

"I hurt. I m-miss him so bad. M-my heart aches for…" She crumpled as if an invisible force had pulled her life's plug.

"No, no, no…" He dropped to his knees, feeling Emily's carotid. Weak, but still there. Terrified for her, he shot into action by calling 9-1-1 on the kitchen landline. "Stay with me."

"Nine-one-one. How may I direct your call?"

"M-my sister. I think she may have accidentally overdosed."

"I'm sending paramedics. The address I have on file for this number is…" She rambled off a number Jed hadn't heard in a while but thought sounded right. "Is your sister conscious?"

"No."

"Is she breathing?"

"Yes—but her inhalations are slow."

"Okay, sir. I'll let the paramedics know. Please stay on the line."

Each minute had stretched into an eternity.

Seated on the kitchen floor, cradling Emily's head in his lap, Jed had held the cordless phone in the crook of his neck, giving the operator updates as needed.

Finally, strobing ambulance lights sliced the night.

And then he'd left the calm of Ollie's, the shelter of Camille's voice, to once again thrust himself into the heart of his sister's tragic storm.

Frenzied ER nurses and doctors shouting medical directions in what to his soldier's ears sounded like a foreign language.

Then came hours of silence, with him assuming his sister would be fine. Only she wasn't. And now, here he stood, hands rammed in his jean pockets, unsure what to do or say.

"Em…" He'd finally reached her bedside.

He tried holding her hand, but it was cold and stiff, reminding him in no uncertain terms that she was well and truly gone.

Jed wasn't a crier, but found himself hunched over her, sobbing like one of the babies she'd left behind.

"W-why?" he asked, trying to make sense of the illogical. "What am I supposed to tell Mom? Your daughters? I want—*have*—to believe this was an accident. But then I remember the hollow look in your eyes and it scares me. Did you want to be with Chase more than the rest of us?"

He stared at her for the longest time, feeling like an idiot upon realizing he was waiting for her to answer.

Jed needed to kick something. Punch a wall. But this was neither the time nor place.

Now was the time when he wished he could be more of a touchy-feely sort. He needed to say—do—something deep or profound. But he had nothing. Where his heart used to beat with love and pride for his sister and her little family, was now an empty shell.

He wanted to believe Emily's death had been an accident, but what if it hadn't? What if she truly had been so overcome by grief that not even the bond of motherhood could override her depression?

Jed had come here to help, but instead, his sister died on his watch. What did that say about him?

Eyes welling again, he pressed his lips tight, fighting this fresh onslaught of emotion.

With three infant nieces now in his sole charge, taking time to grieve would be a luxury he didn't have.

"Rest." He kissed Emily's cold forehead, then took a step back. "I promise… Your girls will never want for anything—especially love."

After signing paperwork and insurance forms and speaking with a funeral home representative about the impossible topic of body storage until after Jed's mother could be found, he finally left the hospital and walked on autopilot to Emily and Chase's SUV.

The sky above shone a deep cerulean blue.

The only reason he knew the color was because of the summer he'd fallen so hard for Camille. With her leg broken, she'd passed time with her new hobby of painting. She'd always been begging him to drive her to an Aspen art supply store for more of her favorite shade.

Did she still paint?

He suddenly needed to know.

The vehicle's air was stuffy and too hot, and smelled of soured baby formula and something sweet and no doubt sticky.

He started the engine and cranked the AC, but otherwise couldn't seem to move. His limbs were as frozen as his heart.

Leaning forward, he rested his head against the sunscorched steering wheel. The black leather stung his forehead, but he didn't care. Couldn't care.

All his capacity for caring remained in that sad, sterile hospital room with his once vibrant sister.

Lord, how he wished he hadn't screwed things up with Camille. She'd always been good in a crisis. That time his mother's Pomeranian, Cupcake, had been eaten by a coyote—she'd known exactly how to console his mom by giving her a tray of pretty pink-frosted cupcakes along with a matching headstone of sorts that Ollie had helped her make. She'd painted the wooden sign pink, adding the dog's name and the dates she'd lived, along with a brief poem she'd written.

Camille was a good person.

And I'm not?

Not particularly. The things Jed had seen and done had hardened him to a point that he no longer recognized himself. Right now, he should be speeding back up the mountain to care for his sister's newborns.

The only thing he wanted to do? Point the SUV toward Coronado and hop the first C-130 bound for anywhere in the world besides Marigold, Colorado, and Camille and more responsibility than he could comfortably handle.

Chapter 3

"Shouldn't Jed be back by now?" At almost noon, Camille sat on the living room floor on the quilt she'd spread in front of the TV. Not sure what to do with three babies while her grandfather watched a Western, she tried keeping the fussy critters in their makeshift corral. "Hope Em's going to be okay."

"She's fine. You know how hospitals are. Taking too damn long for every damned thing—that way they can suck all the money out of you at the same time they suck your blood."

"Cynical much?" She cocked her head. Not that she had room to talk, considering her own negative world views.

A baby tried escaping, but Camille snagged her around her tiny waist. She wished she'd paid closer attention the previous night when Jed had run through the girls' names. She'd been so distracted by his call last night—the first in years—that she hadn't thought to ask then, either. In her current state of too little sleep and too much worry for her friends, it bothered her, not knowing such a basic fact. She reached for her cell nearby and tried dialing Jed's number, now in her phone from last night. No answer.

"Do you have Emily's number?" she asked her grandfather. She used to, but her friend recently changed it and her cellular service provider.

"Maybe? If I do, it would be in that blue spiral notebook I keep by the phone." The landline phone that had sat on the kitchen counter long enough for the rubber pads to have worn off the old-fashioned rotary dial base.

"Thanks. Mind keeping an eye on those two?" Camille rose, taking the runaway cutie for a ride on her hip. Her sisters looked like upside-down green and yellow turtles while examining each other and their toes.

"Sure, sure…" Her grandfather waved her along. "Though I still say it's a waste of energy to worry."

"Duly noted." Camille rolled her eyes.

Sifting through her pack rat grandfather's papers was always an adventure. He kept every receipt and jotted mining notes as if he were a full-time college student. About two inches deep into a foot-tall pile, she unearthed the blue notebook.

Inside were quotes from John Wayne to Oprah. Recipes for Italian Seasoned Popcorn and Candy Corn Rice Krispies Treats. Eventually, she noticed phone numbers scrawled in the margins but none for Emily.

Sighing, she gave the baby in her arms a jiggle. "Hope your mom's okay. Your uncle, too."

The infant stared, her big blue eyes wide and inquisitive. As if looking at the stranger holding her wasn't providing enough information, she jabbed her tiny hand into Camille's hair, curling her fingers into a fist.

"Ouch." Camille laughed. "You're strong."

"So is Emily." Carrying the other two babies, her grandfather entered the room. "Stop worrying. She'll be fine."

"I know..." Absentmindedly nuzzling the crown of the baby's head, Camille stared out the kitchen window at snow-covered Meyer's Peak and shimmering, aptly named Glass Lake. She'd planned on packing a lunch and hiking there today. Looks like she'd need to put it off for another time.

The morning feeding led to the afternoon feeding.

With her grandfather asleep in his recliner and John Wayne's *The Quiet Man* playing not so quietly on TV, Camille had almost convinced Baby #3 to close her eyes when the sound of a car engine outside jarred the tiny creature into an outraged howl that was loud enough to rouse her sisters.

"Crap..." Camille sighed. Motherhood was no joke.

Thank God, Jed and Emily were back to take over.

With the two loudest little ladies in her arms, she went to the door to greet her neighbors. With poor Chase gone, Camille vowed to be there for her friend as much as possible. It wouldn't take just a village to raise three newborns, but a thriving metropolis.

A quick glance over her shoulder showed Baby #1 cuddling with her fuzzy pink blanket and stuffed unicorn. Eyes blessedly closed—*yes*.

On her brief trek to the front door, Camille narrowly avoided tripping over stuffed bunnies and teething rings and the swing she had yet to assemble.

She opened the door, expecting to find Emily and Jed exhausted but otherwise okay.

The sight she encountered filled her with instant cold dread. Her stomach knotted.

Jed sat behind the wheel—alone.

But that didn't necessarily mean anything.

Em could still be at the hospital. Or lying down in the roomy SUV's backseat. There were any number of logical explanations for Jed returning on his own. She wanted to hear one of them. *Now.* Her runaway pulse rocketed to the worst-case scenario and that wouldn't help any of them.

With the babies held snuggly on her hips, she carefully navigated the porch stairs. The day was bright and sunny—not a trace of wind, with temperatures in the downright-balmy high seventies. Conifer-laced air reminded her why she loved not just Colorado, but her grandfather's special corner of the world.

"Hey…" She slowly approached the car.

Jed still wasn't moving.

Alarm bells rang, but she shut them down.

"Jed?" she asked through the closed car window. "Everything all right? Long night?"

When, even after her questions, he still didn't so much as glance her way, she could no longer deny nothing about this scene was normal.

She took the liberty of trying to open his door, but it was locked. The engine was still running.

"Jed?" She landed a light kick to the door. "How about killing the motor?"

As if on autopilot, he at least complied with that small request.

"Good," she said with a tight nod, slipping into crisis-management mode. "Very good. Now, unlock the door for me. I need to make sure you're okay."

He pressed a button, resulting in an electronic click.

It was an awkward move with two tiny infants pressed to her chest, but she managed to fit her hand into the handle and squeeze the latch.

With the door open, she found Jed wearing the same clothes he had last night—khakis and a Go Navy T-shirt that hugged his remarkable chest in all the right places. Given the circumstances, whatever they might be, the observation was in incredibly poor taste.

Slipping back into professional mode, she noticed his eyes. Red-rimmed and bloodshot to the extreme. Had it even been safe for him to drive the winding mountain road?

"Jed…" She repositioned the babies to cup his forearm. "I'm afraid to ask. But Emily? Is she okay?"

He shook his head. Covered his face with his hands.

"She's still at the hospital? That's all right. She's been through a lot—losing Chase. Caring for the girls. Any new mom would be overwhelmed. In fact—"

"She's gone."

Camille frowned. "Like, her doctor transferred her to another facility? Denver? Salt Lake City?"

"She's *gone*."

Dawning was slow to come, but when it did, the terrifying jolt was as shocking as if she'd been electrocuted. *No.* Chase and Emily both gone? *No, no, no.* The thought was inconceivable. She refused to believe it.

One glance at Jed's defeated posture and blank features proved his statement true. "I can't find my mom," he said. "I need to find her. She needs to know."

"Of course. I have friends on the Miami force who will pull strings to track her down."

He nodded. "Thanks."

"Let's get you inside. You need coffee. A good meal and rest."

"I can't eat."

"You will eat. Come on…" She gestured for him to exit the car. No doubt in shock, he couldn't seem to un-latch the seat belt, but with the babies in her arms, she wasn't much help. Eyeing their car carriers still buckled into the back, she opened the rear door, set each baby securely in their seats, then rushed back to Jed, who needed her far worse.

She reached past him, freeing him from the belt be-fore easing the gearshift into Park. Thank goodness, his foot was already on the brake.

"Come on…" She held out her arms and he fell into them.

How many nights had she'd lain awake, dreaming of holding him again? But never like this. Not under these awful circumstances.

Bracing herself to bear his weight, she cradled his head into the crook of her neck, smoothing his too short hair. She knew from the news that oftentimes SEALs wore full beards and long hair to blend with locals. How long had it been since Jed had been stateside from his latest overseas mission?

He didn't cry, just held her, clung to her as if rely-ing on her strength to carry him through. Didn't mat-ter that they'd ended their once loving relationship on the ugliest of notes.

The past ceased to matter when the present hurt this badly.

In that moment, he needed her. She needed him.

All the heinous death she'd witnessed, all the crimes

so vicious they might have been committed by animals as opposed to humans, came roaring back.

Jed might have held back tears, but she couldn't. Not when sweet Emily and Chase were gone, yet monsters roamed free.

Wasn't fair.

Didn't make sense.

Instead of feeling more at peace with her place in the world, she felt more at war. Three innocent babies were now without parents. A brother without his sister. A mother without her daughter. Senseless tragedy piled atop tragedy and for what?

If there was a God, she'd be hard-pressed to find evidence of His existence...

Jed was slow to wake.

When his eyes fully opened, he rubbed sandpaper from them, gazing about his sister's sun-flooded living room. It was the same, but different. And then it all came rushing back.

"What happened?" one of the paramedics asked. He was a mountain of a man with a bushy red beard and hair.

Since Emily's situation seemed more time sensitive, Jed let the three tenors—his nieces—do what they did best. Make noise. "She lost her husband a couple weeks ago and was prescribed tranquilizers to help cope. I think she may have accidentally taken more than her prescribed dosage."

The two-man crew pushed him aside to lift Emily onto a collapsible stretcher. Within a few minutes, she'd been taken from the house and hefted into the ambulance's service bay. While the red-haired mountain of a man started an IV, the slimmer of the two paramedics thrust a clipboard filled with forms at Jed.

"Are you a relative?"

"Her brother."

"Good. I'll need you to sign for consent to treatment."

Jed did.

"Does she have insurance?"

"I'm sure, but I'll have to find her card."

"You can show it at the hospital."

Nodding, Jed asked, "Which one?"

"Aspen Valley. Add an emergency contact number beneath your signature."

Done.

"Want to ride along?"

"Can't. My sister has newborn triplets. As soon as I find someone to care for them, I'll head that way."

"We gotta go!" The mountain man shouted loudly enough to be heard over the rioting babies. "Her pulse is tanking."

"Wait—what does that mean?" Jed chased the driver out the front door. "You can help her, right?"

The man ignored him in favor of closing the back doors, then climbing behind the wheel.

Before Jed made it off the porch, the ambulance sped away, lights flashing.

Dust rose from the dirt drive, swirling in the pale porch lights.

Rubbing his tearing eyes with his thumb and forefingers, Jed barely recalled earlier that afternoon when Ollie and Camille had helped him into the passenger seat of his sister's SUV. He'd sat there in a daze while they'd loaded his nieces and their gear.

There was a vague recollection of the girls squalling

while Camille shuffled him inside the too-still house, leaving him on the sofa while she must've gotten the triplets squared away.

Now, he eased upright, wincing at the sharp pain in his forehead.

"Take it easy…" Camille perched on the sofa's end, lifting his feet onto her lap.

"What time is it?"

"Ten in the morning. You slept through the rest of yesterday and through the night. I just put your nieces down for a nap."

He groaned. "I'm sorry. You shouldn't have let me sleep that long."

"You obviously needed the rest. Coffee?"

"Please." He should get it himself, but the trek to the kitchen struck him as insurmountable.

"Sit tight. I'll be right back."

He closed his eyes and sighed.

Directly across from his position on the sofa was the fireplace. A fire crackled and popped, lacing the air with sweet wood smoke. Since his arrival a few days earlier, making the fire had been one of his chores. Emily had always loved a cheery fire. *Had.* Seemed inconceivable that he think of his little sister in the past tense.

"Hungry?" Camille asked, after handing him a steaming mug.

"No, thank you."

She settled in the armchair across from him, drawing her legs alongside her. He'd forgotten how tiny she was. How beautiful. How sunlight caught honey gold strands in her long, chestnut hair. How her hazel eyes turned darker or lighter depending on her mood. He used to tease that she was his lil' snack. She'd claimed the endearment drove her nuts, but he'd also caught her grinning about it on more than one occasion.

"Now that you're alert…" Clasping her hands around her own steaming coffee mug, she said, "We have stuff to discuss. Along with a lot of concerned friends, your mom called last night, but she's too far into the bush to easily get a charter flight. She didn't want me to wake you, but asked that we hold off on Emily's memorial service until she gets home."

"Of course."

"While you were out, there was a steady stream of Emily and Chase's friends. They brought casseroles and cakes and three hams."

Jed's head swam. His chest ached as if he couldn't drag in enough air. The fact that he'd lost his brother-in-law hadn't even fully sunk in. How could his sister now be gone, too?

He was beyond grateful to Camille for dealing with the well-wishing visitors. They would have been one more issue he couldn't have handled.

"I know this is probably the last thing you want to think about," she said, "but when you were here—with your sister—did she have any tricks for how to tell the girls apart?"

"Yeah, they're color coded." A wistful smile toyed with the corners of his lips. "Allie is pink. Callie is yellow. Sallie is pistachio—not that I know what that is?"

"Greenish, but pale."

"Got it."

"Funny," she said with a sad smile of her own, "I was thinking we could write their names on their feet bottoms with a Sharpie, but the whole color thing makes more sense. This is probably why I'll never be a mom."

"Don't be so hard on yourself. Way I remember it, every horse, goat, dog and kitten on this mountain adored you."

She bowed her head.

"For what it's worth, I am sorry about how things went down between us."

"You already said that. Besides, water under the bridge."

Only he got the feeling it wasn't—for either of them.

From the nursery came the faint sound of crying.

"Break time's over," she said with false cheer.

"I'll help." He pushed himself upright, at first unsteady, but he soon regained his balance.

The babies were so young, Emily hadn't yet trusted them with a sitter, meaning that if he and Camille couldn't figure out how to handle the rowdy crew, he didn't even have numbers to call.

The only living soul on this mountain besides him and the girls, and now Camille, was cantankerous Ollie. Back when Jed lived out here and Camille's grandmother had died, the grizzled old goat had displayed the charm of a stomach flu combined with the manners of a pissed-off rattler. Still, his granddaughter had turned out great, which meant he at least knew enough about kids to have raised one to adulthood. That automatically put him ahead of Jed in the parenting department.

Jed passed Camille on the stairs to find all three babies screaming in the nursery. "This is how they earned their nicknames. I call them the three tenors."

"Fitting."

"I'm here," he said to the huffy princesses in their pink palace of a sun-flooded room. Pink floral walls served as the backdrop for big paned windows with pink curtains and white trim. A fluffy white area rug covered hundred-year-old pine floors. "What's the problem?"

He picked up Callie, to find her diaper dry. The instant he held her, she quieted, aside from a few offended huffs over having waited so long.

Picking up Sallie went the same. Dry diaper. Highly offended by the wait time between start of tears and service.

Allie was another story. Wet and poopy diaper.

Sigh. He wiped her down and wrapped her in a fresh diaper as efficiently as if he was packing a parachute—at least that was the plan. But his big fingers always made a mess of the sticky tabs and he ended up gluing one to the baby's belly, resulting in more screams when he removed it as gently as possible.

She was still huffing with pouty-faced fury when he lifted her into his arms, then scooped up the other two again. Though holding all three at once was a challenge, until they grew, it was doable.

"You're seriously good at this." Arms crossed, rubbing her hands along her upper arms, Camille asked, "Did you and your wife have kids?"

"Nope."

"Totally none of my business, but why not?"

"Long story." He had plenty of time to tell her everything, but the whole miserable failure was too humiliating.

He could ask her why, in the years they'd been apart, she'd never married, but this didn't seem like the right time.

"Want to pack up this crew and get out of here?" he suggested.

"Like, go to town?"

"I was thinking more of a hike. I need to clear my head. None of this makes sense. Your being here instead of my sister. The two of us not having seen each other for a decade, yet here we are changing diapers."

"I know what you mean." She took Allie from him, cradling her close. "This is crazy. How we both always talked about having kids, but never did. Yet here we are, years later, with more babies than anyone could possibly handle."

"True…"

He plopped the other two tenors into Sallie's crib, then grabbed diaper bags, loading them with supplies. Holy hell, he'd packed gear for a six-month stint in Mogadishu that hadn't taken this long.

Faster and faster he shoved diapers and onesies and stuffed animals into a pink-striped bag until Camille placed her hand on his forearm.

"Stop."

He froze upon the realization that her touch hit him like an electrical jolt.

"You're acting possessed by demons you can't fix. Emily and Chase are gone. No amount of baby paraphernalia you cram into that bag will change the fact."

"You don't understand. I can't stay in this house." With the backs of his hands he swiped stupid tears from the sides of his eyes. "Everywhere I look, I see Chase helping Emily hang the giraffe mobile. I see the mantel photo of all five of them visiting the giraffes at the Denver Zoo—the babies so small they probably couldn't even see the animals from their stroller. Em and Chase hanging this god-awful pink-striped wallpaper—both of them with paste in their hair. How could this have happened? Even worse, I can't stop wondering if my sister actually missed Chase to such a degree that she chose to check out."

"You mean take her own life?" Camille gulped.

He nodded.

"No. I have to believe her death was accidental. Anything else is unthinkable. She wouldn't purposely have left her babies."

"Hope you're right."

She took half as much out of the diaper bags as he'd placed in. "Gramps gifted Chase and your sister with an off-road stroller that has chunky, all-terrain tires. The girls love it, so they won't need toys. We'll take a few diapers and wipes, toss in formula, then be off, okay?"

"Sounds good. Hey…" Not thinking, just acting on pure instinct when she turned to leave the room, he cupped his hand around her upper arm. "Thanks. For everything. Not just being here and helping, but—" he bowed his head "—for talking me down."

"No worries," she said. "I told you I'd be here for the duration and I will. All we have to do is care for the girls till your mom gets back, and then we're home free, right?"

Chapter 4

Famous last words.

For Camille, settling three screaming infants into the stroller wasn't a simple task but a siege. Allie had been quiet and smiley but then soiled her diaper and needed to be cleaned before being placed back in her spot at the stroller's rear. Sallie sat in the center, apparently screaming just to be screaming. She wasn't hungry, her diaper was clean, she didn't need burping—just apparently wanted a good, long cry.

Join the club.

Could the infant be missing her mom?

Callie screamed so loudly her cheeks turned splotchy and swollen and red enough that Camille worried they may need to phone the pediatrician's number that Emily had kept on a magnet mounted to the side of the fridge. But then Jed found the oversize lip-shaped pacifier she'd dropped to the stroller's net floor, brushed it off, popped it back in her mouth, then voilà, only one screaming infant to go.

"What do you think's wrong with her?" Camille asked.

"Hard to say. Could be anything from gas to hunger to missing her parents." He plucked her from the stroller. "Chase had a baby backpack sling contraption. How about I hold her in that, and you push the other two?"

"Sure. Anything to help."

Fifteen minutes and another diaper change later, they were off.

Camille encouraged Jed to take the lead down the rugged path. It was plenty wide enough for the stroller, but rocky and steep in spots, which he helped her and her charges to pass. Douglas fir and ponderosa pine towered over them, smelling pungent and fresh and far from what she'd imagined had been the scents Jed had been subjected to at the hospital.

They wound higher and higher up the mountain, over a meandering stream and around car-sized boulders and switchbacks with drop-offs steep enough that she wasn't sure it was such a great idea to even have the girls along for the ride.

Even worse, dark clouds rolled in from the west.

Jed climbed as if driven by forces she couldn't begin to understand.

But then maybe she did?

Her entire reason for escaping Miami for this mountain was to elude her own demons. They might not revolve around the death of her loved ones—though she did grieve for Emily and Chase—but in her own way, she'd loved each and every child whose case she'd fought so hard to solve.

The steeper the climb, the thinner the oxygen, the more her lungs burned and chest heaved. She wasn't yet used to the altitude.

All three babies howled, but then grew eerily silent.

"Jed, we have to have gained three or four thousand feet in elevation. For the girls' safety, we should head down."

He kept climbing. "I have to get to the top."

"Why?" She stopped, folding over to catch her breath while bracing her hands on her knees.

"I just do!" His tone was harsh enough to startle Sallie from her eerie sleep into a full-blown wail.

"Then give me Sallie and you go self-destruct on your own."

"I'm not self-destructing."

"Whatever the hell label you'd like to put on it, this mountainside isn't safe in a storm."

Lightning cracked and thunder boomed.

"That's it," she said. "Finish this mission—or death wish—on your own." She took Sallie from him then tucked her into the stroller and fastened her safety harness. "We'll hopefully see you back at the house."

She'd already gone a good fifty feet down the trail when he called, "Camille, hold up!"

"Why?"

"Because you're right."

Once again, she froze. Or was that hell freezing over? Had the great Jed Monroe just admitted he was wrong?

Lightning again cracked.

Back to her, hands on his hips, he looked to the sky.

"I thought if I climbed high enough, far enough, I could escape this pain. Why do people I love keep dying? Em and Chase. Both of our dads. Your grandmother. So many of my SEAL brothers. Sometimes it feels like I'm the last man standing."

"But you're not…" Her voice fell soft enough to barely reach him. "You have me." *At least for a little while.*

"But I don't deserve you—never did."

A few cold raindrops fell and then more and more, until they were under a full-on deluge. Good thing the stroller had a cover.

"Take this." He shrugged off the backpack, then took the stroller from her, heading down the mountain in record time.

Once they'd reached the two-story ranch house, the rain had turned to snow and they were all shivering. The poor babies had turned pale.

"We need to get them in warm water," Camille said.

"Agreed."

He took Sallie and Callie, charging to the upstairs hall bathroom. He set them on their backs on the thick white rug, then turned the tub's taps, testing the lukewarm water on his wrist.

Camille had followed.

"I'm such a screwup," he mumbled. "My first official day as an uncle-turned-temporary-dad and I almost killed them. And for what? A misguided attempt to literally run from old problems, and the new ones that aren't going anywhere for a good eighteen years. And my nieces aren't problems, but Emily's most cherished possessions."

"You have to stop beating yourself up." Camille removed the trio's hats, sweaters and onesies before tucking three baby bathtubs into the rising water. Once she'd retested it with her wrist, she removed diapers and settled the babies in the pleasantly warm water.

"You're not a dad, but an uncle. There's a huge difference. Once your mom gets home, she'll take over. Until then, all we can do is the best we can do. Playing devil's advocate, since this is spring in the Rockies, next time we venture out with newborns in tow, we need to pack for all weather contingencies, from a blizzard to a heat wave."

"Good call." He sat back on his haunches and sighed. "Sorry."

"For what?" She used a plastic cup on the edge of the tub to scoop water for wetting the babies' hair. Pink had already returned to their cheeks. Allie and Sallie closed their eyes, sporting tiny grins. Callie scrunched her mouth into a frown that threatened tears. "Your meltdown?"

"Yeah. It was stupid. Reckless. Thanks for bringing back my sanity."

"Anyone with you would have done the same."

She glanced over her shoulder and caught him shrugging.

"Do you think Emily did it on purpose?" he asked. "Killed herself?"

"Absolutely not." Camille lied because she sensed he needed the reassurance. She'd seen horrible, unthinkable acts committed for far less meaningful reasons. Emily and Chase had shared the sort of love Camille had never believed possible—at least not after her breakup with Jed. It wasn't too far of a stretch to believe Emily literally hadn't been able to live without her husband.

"Good. I don't think so, either."

Since the babies were already in the tub, Camille washed their hair and tiny bodies. The darker Callie's expression grew, the faster Camille finished the infant's scrub. Done, she said to Jed, "I've got a customer for your drying station."

Thick towel in hand, he rose onto his knees, reaching past and around her to grab the squirming, crying baby. In the process, Camille's shoulder brushed against his. After all this time apart, why was the old electric spark still there? Why did she crave his taste more than chocolate?

It wasn't fair.

They could have had it all until he'd thrown it—*them*—away.

"Shh…" he soothed, wrapping the infant, then holding her, rocking her, cooing to her with a tenderness Camille wouldn't have believed if she weren't seeing it with her own eyes. "I miss your momma, too."

Now that the two formerly smiley babies heard their sister crying, they followed suit. Camille had always dreamed of having children—even gone so far as to wish for Jed's sons or daughters—but one at a time would have been preferable. Caring for three newborns was madness. Could Emily have been suffering from not only grief, but postpartum depression?

With all three ladies wailing, there was no more time for thought—only action.

Camille and Jed formed an assembly line, drying, lotioning, diapering, then dressing the girls in their color-coded onesies.

With the trio warm and dry, but still unhappy, Camille asked, "Think we should feed them?"

"It's early, but worth a try."

Jed carried Allie and Callie to the kitchen.

Camille, with Sallie in her arms, trailed behind.

The crying seemed to have taken a life of its own, like a ghostly monster shrouding them all in gray.

"I'll put this one in her carrier," Camille said, "then make the bottles. You might try jiggling? That worked with one of my coworker's babies."

"Right. I'll give it a go."

While he walked and jiggled, Camille opened a fresh can of premade formula, warmed it, then fitted disposable liners over three bottles before filling them, then screwing on the tops.

"Ready!" she called.

"In the den!" Jed shouted above the racket.

Snow had turned to dime-sized hail. Howling wind pounded it against the old paned windows hard enough for Camille to fear they might break.

In the den that Chase had used for his man cave, with his two charges propped in opposite corners of the sofa, Jed built a fire in the stone hearth.

"That fire feels awesome," she said with a shiver. "Good call."

"Glad you like it. This room warms faster than the living room."

Landing in the overstuffed red sofa's center, Camille managed to hold Allie on her lap, propping her bottle with a throw pillow. The baby sucked as if she'd been starving. Even cutting the screams' volume by a third helped. She reached for Callie, leaning her against her ribs and under her arm. With her bottle propped with another pillow, and the baby suckling with huffing grunts, Camille repeated the drill one last time until the only sounds remaining were the catching fire's soft crackle above the hail and howling wind.

"Whew," she said. "That was intense."

"No kidding." After adding logs to the fire, Jed joined her, relieving her of two of her charges. His size made it a breeze for him to cradle both his nieces at once, but during the trade-off their bottles fell.

Instant tears were just as quickly stopped when Camille fitted the bottles back into the girls' mouths.

"Thanks," Jed said. "We make a good team."

I always thought so. Swallowing an unexpected and unwanted knot in her throat, Camille forced a smile.

He arched his head back and sighed. "None of this feels real. A few days ago I was on base, running landing drills. Now…" There was no need for him to finish the thought, since they both knew where it led.

"Was it everything you'd hoped it would be?" *Was it worth leaving me?*

"The navy?"

"Yeah."

"I have a great life. Lots of friends. What happened between us was—" he blanched "—unfortunate. But you know what they say. Shit happens."

I never said that. I said I loved you and you walked away.

"Yeah." The knot in her throat returned.

She generally wasn't one to hold grudges, so why was it so hard to let go of Jed's offenses? Especially when they'd both been at fault for their relationship not so much even falling apart, so much as evaporating. She'd had college to finish at Florida State and her dream of becoming a police detective—not because the work would be in any way satisfying, but because her father had been killed in cold blood and his murderer never found. Camille couldn't bear another family facing that injustice.

The pity was that she soon learned solving murders was too much like fixing a broken dam by poking your finger in the hole.

The water, the killings, never stopped. The only thing she'd accomplished along her chosen path was losing Jed.

"You apologized last night—for what happened. Between us. But I was just as much at fault."

"Let's not get into it." He shifted, wincing as if in physical pain. "Like you said, water under the bridge."

"I know, but it looks like we'll be spending a lot of time together—at least until your mom gets home. I don't want there to be awkwardness hanging between us."

"I didn't think there was."

Why had she shown her cards?

Are you crazy? she longed to shout. Didn't he feel the spark every time they touched? Considering the fact that circumstances had forced them together, she couldn't be sparking every time he was near. Not only was it inappropriate, given his nieces were now parentless, but as soon as his mom showed up, he would return to California, to his life that consisted of nothing but violence. Sure, he might be fighting on the side of good, but that wouldn't make a knock on her door with strangers telling her the man she loved had been shot any easier.

She glanced down to find Callie had drifted off.

Outside, the hail had transitioned back to snow.

Gotta love spring in Colorado.

"I'm sorry your marriage didn't work out."

"That's random." His two charges still suckled with gusto. Their grunts were the only sounds rising above the crackling fire.

"I suppose. Seeing you again—I, well…" Where did she even start? Why hadn't she asked him about something not half as explosive, like politics or religion? Nothing hurt worse than remembering their past. "Well, being back here, seeing you, it all reminds me of… You know. When you married only a few months after we—"

"My marriage was doomed from the start." He lifted his gaze from the babies to lock stares with her. "The only reason I still think about Alyssa at all is because we still run in the same social circle. In reality…"

Camille's breath caught in her throat.

Had his eyes always been so blue? Had the slight cleft in his chin that she used to kiss grown deeper or was the shadow of his stubble playing tricks with her broken heart?

"This is embarrassing as hell to admit," he said, "but at the time I made my vows, all I wanted was to stop missing you."

"So you married a stranger?" *Was I that easily replaced?*

"Like I said, sounded good at the time."

Sounds stupid.

But who was she to judge? How many times had he begged her to marry him? How many times had she turned him down?

"Since we're on this hike down memory lane, how about you? Anyone serious?"

"A few times I thought things were, but the job kept getting in the way."

"Did it help?"

"What do you mean?"

"Finally becoming a detective? Did it help banish the hurt from what happened to your dad?"

"Nope." She dropped her gaze, twirling one of Allie's downy curls. If anything, it had made her issues with losing her father infinitely worse.

"Hate hearing that. I only ever wanted the best for you."

"Same." Their gazes locked again, propelling her back in time. Back to when she could tell his every mood with one glance. Now they were for all practical purposes strangers who'd come full circle. They'd become friends, sweethearts, lovers, enemies, and now back to friends again—at least, she hoped they were.

Sallie had drifted off. Her bottle fell from her mouth. Thankfully, Jed caught it before the motion spooked her into more tears.

"Too early for a nap?" he asked.

"For them or us?"

"Both." He laughed.

"We owe it to ourselves to try."

A few minutes later, they'd settled the girls into their cribs, tucked them beneath fluffy pink covers, then tip-toed back to the den's crackling fire.

"If you want," he said, "why don't you head back to your grandfather's?"

"Trying to get rid of me?" She eased onto the sofa, cuddling beneath the nubby earthen-toned afghan Emily had knitted.

"Lord, no. I need you. But the last thing I want is for you to feel obligated to stay."

"I'm exactly where I want to be. Gramps usually isn't home from his mine till six or so. I'll need to make him dinner and make sure he takes his meds. After that, I'll come back."

"That's a lot of work."

"So is caring for three newborns."

"True." He sighed, taking the corner opposite hers. Once upon a time he might have stretched alongside her, resting his head on her lap while she stroked his hair. She wished at the time she'd given more care to preserving their memories—especially the seemingly trivial moments she'd taken for granted. The times when doing nothing had meant *everything*.

"I'm worried about how Mom will cope," Jed murmured.

"I'll help. I have no plans to return to Miami anytime soon."

"That would be great. Maybe we could set up a more formal arrangement. I could pay you a salary."

"If I had the energy to move, that asinine suggestion deserves a smack."

"Why? I meant it as a compliment. You're good with my nieces. You deserve to be paid for your services."

"What I deserve…" She bristled. "…is to be treated like a friend and not a stranger." Her cheeks reddened upon remembering that it had been only a few minutes since she'd been the one labeling them strangers.

"Sorry. The last thing I want is to bicker."

"We're not. I'm merely explaining that it's an insult to think I want to be reimbursed for helping care for the infants of two of my oldest—*now dead*—friends."

"Message received." Holding up his hands in surrender, he said, "The subject will never be brought up again."

Outside, lightning flashed.

Thunder boomed.

Camille held her breath, praying their charges slept through the rowdy weather.

Only when a few minutes passed without lightning or tears did she dare exhale. And then her eyelids felt impossibly heavy. "Are you as tired as I am?"

"I think so?" He didn't raise his head from the sofa's backrest, merely rolled it till his weary gaze met hers.

He faintly smiled.

So did she.

Being back on the same page, even about their mutual exhaustion, felt right.

"Wanna take a nap?" she asked.

"Yes, but I'm not sure I can move."

"No need. Let's crash here." She kicked off her sneakers, resting her head on the sofa's arm. The afghan didn't fully cover her, but it felt good on the chilly exposed skin of her arms.

"Good call." He took her suggestion. Literally crashing in place, closing his eyes without moving another muscle.

Moments later, he was not only softly snoring, but had tipped far enough to his right that his head rested on her lower legs. Like old times, he'd draped his arm over her. She knew the action meant nothing, but she couldn't help smiling.

The two of them as a couple might be ancient history, but that didn't stop her from remembering more of the good than the bad.

Naps on rainy afternoons certainly fell under the good.

Still sporting her faint grin, Camille also drifted off. She wasn't sure how long the dreamless sleep had claimed her when lightning struck too close.

The resulting thunder boomed loudly enough to shake the whole house.

Camille's instinctive response was to sit up.

Jed's was to hold her closer. Then he raised his head from where it rested on her outer thigh. The afghan must've slipped, as the side seam of her jeans had imprinted itself on his cheek.

Lord help her, he looked adorable—not the sort of description she supposed a career soldier would appreciate. Lucky for him, she had no intention of sharing. Just enjoying.

"Um, sorry." He released her, rising up as fast as if she had cooties. "Guess I must have..." He waved his hand in a vague sweep of their surroundings.

"No sweat."

"I need you to know I never would have—"

"Jed, stop. I get it. Never in a million years would you willingly touch me again."

He winced. Opened his mouth to stay something, then clamped it shut just as lightning struck again, followed by another house-rattling boom.

In unison, all three babies wailed.

In unison, Camille and Jed groaned.

Camille didn't begrudge leaving the sofa to comfort Emily's girls. What she did resent was not knowing what Jed had been on the verge of saying...

Chapter 5

Thirty minutes later, with the babies happily gumming toys on a quilt Camille had spread near the den's warm fire, Jed asked, "Mind if I duck outside to check the animals?"

She sighed. "I forgot about that other whole side of the family."

"Me, too." Chase had not only helped Emily care for their newborns, but chickens, goats, dozens of cattle and two old mares named Lucy and Ethel. Chase and Emily truly had been living saints, which made losing them so young that much more inconceivable.

"I need to make a schedule." Jed took his jacket from where he'd slung it over the back of a chair and slipped it on, adding his cowboy hat before shoving his feet into his cowboy boots. "It's been almost a full day since I checked their feed and water. Thankfully, Emily told me a neighbor bought their cattle shortly after Chase's death."

"I'm sure the rest of the animals are fine, but just in case, you should go." She shooed him on his way.

Outside, the snow had transitioned to a fine mist.

After the storm's rage, the world had now calmed. *Wish I could say the same for myself.*

His pulse was still erratic from waking to find himself snoozing on Camille's thighs. *Hugging Camille's thighs.*

What the hell?

Even worse, he'd been drowsy enough to have almost admitted how good holding her had felt. He conked his forehead. Clearly, grief and sleep deprivation were taking physical and emotional tolls.

"Hey, ladies and gent," he said inside the chicken coop. They'd run out of food and water and showed their displeasure by converging on him all at once. A few even pecked his cowboy boots. "I know. Sorry. This will never happen again."

Emily had loved her chickens. They all had names, were special breeds and even laid blue and brown eggs. Would they miss her, too?

As soon as the flock was fed and watered, Jed turned on their heat lamp to ward off the afternoon's chill.

Next stop was the goat pen. Same story, different critters.

Though Emily had put making goat cheese on her to-do list, she hadn't yet gotten around to it, thank goodness, meaning her herd of six weren't yet carrying kids.

Before Emily's overdose, Jed had at least moved them from their pasture to the barn, but that had also left them without necessities. He filled one trough with water and the other with hay. He then gave them each a handful of grain, which they greedily gobbled, making his palms slimy in the process.

Since the weather had improved, he left their pen's outer door open, making a mental note to bring them back in for the night. The coyotes up here were no joke.

Out of the barn, he unhooked the chain around the horse pasture's gate, stepped through and closed it behind him.

Lucy and Ethel loved attention, meaning they left their ponderosa pine cover to greet him.

"Hey, ladies." He rubbed their noses. "Are you as put out with me as the rest of the crew?"

Ethel snorted.

"Sorry, gal." They were set enough in their routine to follow him back to the barn's rear entry, where he grabbed them a hay bale, busting it open to flake.

Chase had once told him horses had better internal clocks than humans, meaning they knew when it was time for breakfast, and that today Jed had missed it. This time of year, their high-altitude grazing needed supplementing.

"Things are gonna be different around here…" With the cool afternoon air still, save for the horses' chewing, he stroked their manes. Hard to believe it had been snowing an hour earlier, but that was Colorado for you. If you didn't like the weather, wait ten minutes and it was guaranteed to change. One of the things he loved best about being on his Coronado base was the dependable sun. "I know you two are used to way more attention than you've been getting, but we've got three little hellions up at the house that are major attention hogs."

His speech earned him another snort.

He topped off the galvanized metal water trough, buttoned up the barn, then moseyed back to the house. What did it mean that his chest felt heavy with dread at the mere thought of resuming his new parental responsibilities?

Sure, someday he'd planned on having kids, but with the benefit of nine months to prepare—and maybe just one for starters instead of three.

He hadn't even begun to process losing Emily.

Maybe he never really would?

Once his mom showed up, his CO would expect Jed to return to base. But if he and Camille were struggling as a team, how would his mom be expected to cope on her own with the girls, having just lost her son-in-law and daughter?

Groaning on his way up the front porch steps, he rubbed his hand over two days' stubble.

Time to get over himself and embrace the difficulties of his new temporary life. He'd hire help for his mom and nieces. Camille had offered her support for free.

The selfish bastard in him wishing to escape from this whole untenable situation reasoned why not hire help now? Why not retreat to Cali, where the weather was fine and his most pressing concerns were target practice and shaving a few seconds off night beach-landing times?

Interesting that when Camille turned down his marriage proposal, his first inclination then had also been to run—only not so much toward a destination, but away from the devastation being without her caused. He'd thought his speedy marriage was the solution to his every problem, but he couldn't have been more wrong.

Could he also be mistaken in believing just because he escaped from his nieces that he'd feel better?

In fact, a more probable scenario was that guilt from abandoning Camille or his mother with his three little responsibilities would eat him from the inside.

Camille opened the front door, unwittingly revving his pulse with her smile and half wave. *Damn.* She'd grown infinitely hotter.

"Good, you're back. Since everyone's snoozing in the den, I figured now would be the perfect time to sneak out to cook dinner for Gramps." She ducked back inside to take her purse and keys from the entry hall table. "I'll bring back a plate for you."

"No need."

"What do you mean?" She froze midway out the door.

"I can make a sandwich. There's no reason for you to come back till morning—maybe not even then." *Because I underestimated how much I actually do need you—still want you. But I'm a SEAL. If I'm able to take out entire city blocks of terrorists, I can damn well tackle infant care on my own. As for letting you back into my life, my heart?* Considering how long it had taken to get over her, that was a hard pass on letting her back in.

"Why are you trying to get rid of me?" Arms crossed, she made zero attempt to hide a frown.

"That's the last thing I'm doing." Without hurting her, how did he make her understand that this sudden one-eighty in plans for them to work as a team was all about his personal hang-ups—not her? "If anything, I'm giving you a much-needed break."

"Thanks," she said, with an annoyed jingle of her keys. "But considering how much downtime I've had while caring for my grandfather, who's perfectly capable of caring for himself, I'm happy for the distraction. See you in a couple hours."

Without waiting for his reply, she brushed past him to leave the house and march across the porch.

His body hummed from where she'd brushed against him.

Pressing a hand to his oddly out-of-rhythm heart, he bowed his head and sighed. Too bad his training hadn't covered how to get rid of a woman he very much wanted in his life.

"If Grams saw you sit down to dinner covered in dirt and dust, she'd make you take your plate outside to eat with Earl." Earl was Gramps's best friend and mule.

Camille's grandfather winked. "Then I guess it's a good thing she's no longer with us—bless her gorgeous soul. I loved that woman something fierce, but Lord almighty she could be a harpy."

Ignoring that last comment, Camille kissed the crusty top of his head before delivering him a cold beer, then joining him at the table.

To say she was exhausted would be the understatement of the century. It wasn't even a good exhaustion earned from an extra-hard workout or cleaning the garage. More like a deep-down ache that reached all the way inside her bones, squeezing with enough pressure to make her hurt, but not enough to warrant stopping. Even if it had, it's not like it would've mattered. Jed needed her help with the babies and her grandfather needed a hot meal.

She'd been right to come home. At least this was her temporary home. Her mom wanted her back in

Miami, but Camille didn't see any practical way that could happen. Not with all she'd been through. She'd see a palm tree and it would remind her of the toddler she'd seen—*no*.

Bile rose in the back of her throat.

She'd left Miami for the specific reason to not have those types of memories pop up. She needed them forever banished, along with the anguished mothers' chaotic mix of horrified screams and sobs.

Camille squeezed her eyes shut, following the department shrink's advice to deeply inhale, then count to three before releasing a long, slow exhale.

"You okay?" her grandfather asked, with a bite of chicken fried steak held close to his mouth. "Your mom told me… Well, let's just say I know I'm charming, but you didn't come all this way just to see me."

"True…" Camille looked to her plate, forcing herself to eat, though she wasn't the least bit hungry. She'd fed the babies on and off all day but couldn't remember the last time she'd eaten.

"You ever want to talk about it, your grams always said I was a crap listener, but better than talking to Bonkers—remember him? That old mule we used to have before Earl?"

"The one who ran in circles every time it stormed?"

"That's the one."

She couldn't help but smile at the memory. He'd been a sweetheart. A part of her life she referred to as her Camelot years. Old enough for major, epic make out time with Jed, yet young enough to still be too stupid to realize the two of them as a couple would never last.

Her and Jed's fathers had both still been alive. Their

grandmothers, too. Emily and Chase, a happy couple even back then.

Cupping his hand over hers, her grandfather said, "I'm glad to see that Monroe boy back home." After dropping that conversational bomb, he dug into his mashed potatoes and the white gravy she'd cheated in making, by mixing milk with a store-bought packet.

"He's hardly a boy, Gramps."

"For the way he trampled your poor little heart, he'll always be a boy to me—unless he steps up and does right by you. Which I fully believe he will. Takes some longer than others to recognize their ass from a hole in the ground."

"Gramps!" She dropped her fork onto her grandmother's Blue Willow china with a clatter. "Geez, what's gotten into you? I'm never getting back together with Jed. And it was just as much my decision to call things off."

He stopped shoveling peas long enough to shake his head.

"And anyway, all of that is ancient history. I don't think about it and neither should you." Only that was a lie. Because since encountering Jed again, she'd done nothing but think about him.

About them.

About all the special and lousy times they'd shared.

She and Gramps finished the dinner in somewhat companionable silence, with him thankfully losing himself in his favorite gold mining magazine, while she played Angry Birds on her phone.

When he'd finished, he pushed his chair back. "Since you cooked, I'll wash up."

"That's okay," she said. "I still need to make a plate

for Jed, and you need a shower before tracking mud all over my clean kitchen floor."

"*Your* floor?" He raised his bushy gray eyebrows. "Damn if you aren't sounding more like your harpy grandmother every day." Tears shimmered in his pale blue eyes. "Look like her, too. Pretty as a picture good enough to frame."

"Thanks," she said, even though she couldn't recall a time in recent history when she'd felt less attractive. "I love you."

"Love you, too, peanut. I mean it about that boy. It's good of you to help out the family. It might also be good for you to think about starting a family. He comes from good stock."

Cue eye roll.

Since one of that afternoon's hailstones had somehow lodged itself at the back of her throat, she ignored her grandfather to tackle cleaning the mess from supper.

Camille finished scouring the white kitchen, with its honey-toned pine floors and blue calico curtains. Then she dished up Jed's plate, put away the leftovers, and somehow made it up the stairs to her bedroom, which had been added on when she was a teen.

She needed a shower, too.

By the time she finished, toweled off, dressed and blow-dried her hair, golden sunlight shone through the wall of western-facing windows. The pine floors up here were covered in colorful rag rugs that warmed her toes on chilly mornings. Blue-and-white toile wallpaper made her feel as if she were stepping into the pages of a Jane Austen novel.

The canopy bed added to the room's whimsical charm. Her grandmother had been a huge PBS fan, and while the outside of the house might be log construction, on the inside, she'd designed it to look more like an English cottage.

Calm and beauty ruled.

So why was Camille's pulse racing and her stomach churning?

Jed.

She'd thought they were on the same team when it came to watching the triplets, but when he'd returned from checking on the animals, he'd seemed distant. When she'd suggesting leaving for her grandfather's to make dinner, he'd been a little too enthusiastic about shooing her on her way.

Had waking from their nap to find themselves essentially cuddling bugged him as much as it had her? Not that she hadn't found it pleasant—quite the opposite. But considering how messy her emotions still were from all she'd been through in Miami, the last thing she needed was to toss a man into the mix.

A man?

Ha!

Jed was hardly a generic guy she'd met via work or a dating app. Jed was *the* guy. The one who'd gotten away. And no matter how many other men she'd dated, none of them had ever made her feel one-tenth of the raw attraction she still did with Jed.

Why? What was it about him that had always made her stand a little straighter? Made her heart beat a little faster?

"Cammy!" Her grandfather trudged up the stairs. "Cammy! Where're my Rolaids?"

After forcing a deep breath and smoothing her hair

back into a ponytail, Camille left her room to meet Gramps in the hall.

"*Cammy!* I really need—oh, there you are."

She kissed his cheek. "Your Rolaids are on the side table next to your recliner."

"Nope. Already checked."

"Let's check again." Mostly, he was 100 percent capable of caring for himself, but his eyesight wasn't what it used to be, nor was his memory.

"Okay, but I'm telling you I already…"

By the time he finished his speech about how he had a steel trap mind, she made it to his recliner's side table and back. *Bingo*. His antacids were right where he'd left them, behind his Vick's ointment, tissue box and the TV remote.

She'd snatched them up, then backtracked to meet him at the base of the stairs. "Here you go. Don't take too many."

"Don't tell me what to do." He was supposed to have only two, but being an ornery old goat, he took three. "Where'd you find 'em?"

"On the kitchen counter. You were right."

"Always."

Because she wanted him to think as highly of himself as she did, she swallowed the little white lie. After her grandmother died, he'd told Camille that he wished he'd gone first so he wouldn't be left without her. The notion had broken her heart. But in some ways the sentiment had been a compass for her own life. If she didn't love a man enough to feel as if she'd rather die than lose him, what was the point?

The only guy who'd even come close to stirring that strong of an emotional bond had been Jed. Considering how that relationship had ended in disaster, Camille vowed that from now until he returned to California, she'd keep her shields up where her mishmash of feelings for him were concerned.

"Mmm… That's better." Gramps smoothed his hand across his chest. "Say, you never did tell me how things are going between you and Jed. He hasn't tried any hanky-panky, has he? I'm all for him courting you, but it's too soon for that."

"My virtue is safe." *But I wish it wasn't.*

Turning her back on her grandfather, Camille covered her superheated cheeks with her hands.

Chapter 6

With Camille out of the house, Jed finally felt as if he could breathe.

A long time ago, she had been family.

Now, he couldn't begin to identify what he felt for her, and he was too tired and grief-stricken to care. Only that wasn't entirely true, or she wouldn't still be in his head. Teasing and tormenting and reminding him of happier times when all their loved ones had still been alive.

He released a long, slow exhale.

In the kitchen, he made two roast beef and Swiss sandwiches, wishing he could wash them down with a beer. But with his nieces' nap time ticking away like a time bomb, he figured his night would be best spent sober.

He took his plate, a bag of potato chips and a Coke into the den, where the fire had died to glowing embers.

When setting his meal on the coffee table in front of

the sofa, he missed the table's edge and the soda rolled onto the carpet. He plucked it up, righting it next to his plate, added a few logs to the fire, then checked on the babies.

Allie had kicked off her blanket and Sallie hugged a stuffed pig. Callie startled him when he found her wide-awake, staring at herself in the reflection of the hanging brass fireplace tools.

Trying to buy himself enough time to eat, he slowly backed away before she saw him.

Too late.

Spooked, she lurched, then let loose with a mighty wail.

Callie's cry launched a chain reaction with her sisters, and ten seconds later, all three were screaming at the top of their tiny lungs.

So much for his sandwiches...

Lord, he needed that beer.

Sitting on the floor, he managed to fit all three babies on his lap for a cuddle. After a few minutes of rocking and off-key singing, they quieted.

"This is exactly why I call you guys—or I guess that would be gals—the three tenors."

Three pairs of eyes stared at him in wonder.

"Not sure who they are? Well, your grandmother Barbara loves opera. Remember meeting her the day you were born?"

They gave him their rapt attention.

He laughed. "Glad to see you're taking this seriously. Well, these three guys sang like nobody's business. They were a bit before my time, too, but your grandmother and great-grandmother Paulina—you never got to meet her—used to listen to opera every Saturday while baking. They'd bake bread for the week, and cookies and pastries. The whole time, they'd sing along with these three guys."

His eyes welled from the memory's sudden intensity. How good the kitchen had smelled and how his grandmother had always looked the other way when he'd sneaked a handful of oatmeal cookies from the cooling rack.

He ached for these innocents who would never know their parents. How fortunate he was to have spent time with so much family before they'd passed.

"Anyway… You're my three tenors because you love to sing. Only to me, opera always sounded a little like screaming. You're especially good at that, too."

Allie blew a raspberry.

Callie sniffed and huffed.

Sallie gurgled and cooed.

"When is the last time you ladies ate?" Cupping his forehead, he tried remembering. Had Camille helped him feed before or after the nap that had shattered his last remaining shred of cool where she was concerned?

Before. Definitely before. Otherwise they wouldn't have been able to grab that nap.

"Since you're all wide-awake, what should we do?"

His question earned blank stares.

What did it say about his exhaustion level that he'd halfway expected an answer?

Spying the survival navigation guide he'd been reading before…

He closed his eyes on a rush of the other night's memories. His sister's haunting last words. Dialing 9-1-1. The ambulance's chaotic red and blue strobe.

Pacing the hospital waiting room, assuming Emily would be fine, until learning the awful truth.

He picked up the navigation guide, forcing his pulse to slow. "You ladies are old enough to learn how to find your way home, right?"

He used his shirttail to wipe drool from Sallie's chin. Tough crowd.

He read in a singsong voice from *The U.S. Navy SEAL Survival Handbook* he'd bought online: "'Stay proficient with your map and compass training. Too many people rely solely on a GPS and don't know how to navigate using a map and compass. Everything mechanical will eventually break, and being under a triple canopy in a jungle, or not being able to reach a satellite can cause you...'"

All three babies were out.

"I don't blame you," he whispered. "This thing was written for civilians, but since your uncle Jed was trained by a couple of the authors, I figured I should give it a mercy read. But one valuable nugget of info we've learned is that reading this manual is the perfect sleeping potion. Who needs lullabies when I've got this secret weapon?"

Sleep deprived and inordinately proud of himself, Jed painstakingly placed his nieces back on their comfy quilt palette, pushed himself onto his feet, then crept back to the sofa and his abandoned sandwich.

He sat, took his first bite, chewed and happily sighed.

After swallowing, he reached for his Coke, popped it open, then cussed a blue streak when it exploded like a freaking sugar geyser.

Worse than the syrupy mess coating his T-shirt, hands, arms, sofa and carpet?

All three babies were once again screaming.

"How can I help?" Camille set Jed's foil-wrapped supper on the entry hall table along with her purse and keys, then held out her arms to take Sallie. Or was it Callie? In the heat of the moment, with the triplets red-faced from crying, she'd forgotten the color code.

"That thing I said earlier," he called above the racket, "about how I don't need you? Load of horseshit."

"Emily wouldn't like you cussing around the babies."

"Then she shouldn't have left them with me."

"Jed..." Camille's voice was softer than he deserved. "I can't believe your sister would have ever purposely left her babies. What happened was an accident. A horrible accident."

With all three girls bawling, Camille couldn't be sure her words had even reached him, but if they hadn't, their history, the love she used to have for him—maybe would always have—compelled her to settle the baby she held against her hip, freeing one arm to wrap Jed in a hug.

An upward glance showed him crying, too, but the tears were silent, and she doubted he wanted her to see. He'd been through so much. But then so had she. They were both the walking wounded. As much as it hurt being with him again, it also felt right. As if they'd come full circle.

"Let me help you through this," she said.

He nodded.

"I'm going to make their bottles. And tomorrow, we're going to establish a firm schedule. Sound good?"

Again, he nodded. But this time, sharply looked away. "Their carriers should be around here somewhere. Let me get them contained and I'll give you a hand."

"I'm good," she said. "You try to relax. I'll be back in a sec."

With her mystery baby riding her hip, Camille went to the kitchen, where she prepped three bottles. In under five minutes, she carted the baby and their meals to the den.

Jed paced in front of the fireplace, lightly jiggling his two charges while they screamed loudly enough that veins popped out in their foreheads.

"What's wrong with them?" he asked. "They were fine a little while ago."

"News flash—" she nodded for him to join her on the sofa "—it's not like I have any more parenting experience than you."

Once he'd sat alongside her with a baby stretched out on each knee, she passed him a pair of bottles.

At first, none of the girls seemed interested, but after ten minutes or maybe an hour—the constant screaming made it hard to think, let alone judge time—the infant she held latched on to the bottle's nipple and suckled.

Soon, one more decided to take her bottle.

The decrease in the noise level was beyond a blessing.

When all three babies stopped crying, Camille literally sighed with relief. "Thank God."

"No kidding." He, too, released a long sigh. "Since it hasn't been that long since the last time we fed them, I didn't think they were hungry."

"Who knows? Maybe they needed comfort food?" She traced her baby's furrowed eyebrows. Tears still clung to her long dark lashes. "They're beautiful when they're not crying."

"Yeah..."

"Did you hear me earlier? About your sister?"

"Sure. But I'm so freaking tired. This parenting thing is so new." He arched his head against the sofa cushion much like he had that afternoon. He was so handsome that her breath caught in her throat. The angle of his jaw, shadowed by dark stubble. Eyes as green as ponderosa pine. "I tried calling my mom, but her phone went straight to voice mail."

"There's no telling where she is. Or even if there's power. Her phone could be dead."

"So could she."

"Now you're being melodramatic. She's fine. She'll get here when she can." Camille shifted the baby to her other arm, wincing from the pins and needles in her first one from having held her for too long in the same position. "Tomorrow, once we've established our schedule, everything will look brighter. Tonight, we'll take shifts. That way we'll at least get some sleep."

"Good plan. Thanks."

"You're welcome." In their newfound calm, she noticed the mess on the coffee table. The soggy-looking sandwich and chips. "What happened?"

"Long story. The concise version is that I'm starving, and that goopy mess represents the last of the bread and roast beef."

"Lucky for you I brought chicken fried steak and mashed potatoes. Peas, too."

He groaned. "Heaven on a plate."

"I cheated on the gravy. It's from a mix."

A faint laugh escaped him. "Have you ever tasted what MRE's call gravy?"

She shook her head.

"If you had, you'd know I won't be complaining. Besides, you were always a great cook—just like your mom and grandma."

A warm flush rose up her chest and neck at his praise. "Thanks."

"You're welcome."

"We shared a lot of good times around the table at your gram and gramps's house—here, too."

"Yes, we did."

Their shared glance lasted a little too long.

Both looked away.

"Remember my tenth birthday?" he asked. "When I wanted spaghetti and your mom and my mom both made huge batches?"

"Yes," she said, happy for the smile. "Only they bickered about whose was best and then made you decide?"

"And I couldn't, so I ate heaping bowls of both till I practically popped?"

"Me, too." Holding her hand over her belly, she said, "Is it possible to be hungover from Italian? I still don't like it."

"Same."

Their gazes met again, only this time instead of being awkward, it felt right. Their shared past was so much more than their romance. Before they'd ever been lovers, they'd been friends. She'd give anything to find that camaraderie again.

The baby she held had fallen asleep. The nipple had fallen from her mouth. Formula dribbled down her chin.

Camille used her T-shirt's hem to wipe it clean.

Chuckling, Jed said, "I used my shirt a while ago. Glad to see I'm not the only one crusted in baby goo."

"Wonder where Emily kept her burp cloths?"

"If you're talking about the square things she made with pink flannel and giraffes on one side and towel fabric on the back, there's a stack of them in the nursery. On the changing table's bottom shelf."

"Good to know. Thanks."

"No problem." He gazed down at the two babies he held, with such a tender look of adoration that her throat tightened. "Crazy, isn't it? How when they're kicking up a fuss, I was ready to tear my hair out in frustration. But then when they're sweet and sleepy like this, my heart doesn't feel full enough to hold all of my love."

"Listen to you…" Her lips curved up at the corners. "Turning all poetic on me."

"You know what I mean." He shifted so she couldn't see him, making her sorry for poking fun. What he didn't know was that far from laughing at his tender sentiment, she agreed. And her opinion of him rose that much higher.

The house's ancient landline rang.

Camille froze, waiting to see if the noise woke their sleeping charges.

"Since I'm the only one with a free hand," she said on her way to the kitchen, "I'll get it."

"Thanks. In the meantime, I'll put these two in their carriers."

"Hello?" she said into the handset after the third ring.

"Yes, do I have the residence of Chase and Emily Harrison?"

"Yes. I'm Camille—a neighbor."

"Oh—Camille, this is Baxter Willoughby. Chase and

Emily's attorney. I can't begin to tell you how sorry I was to hear of the family's latest tragedy."

"Thank you…" *But I'm not family.* Not anymore.

"Is Emily's brother available?"

"Sure. Hold on for a sec while I get him." She placed the handset on the kitchen counter, then went in search of Jed, literally running into him on her way to the den.

Chest to chest, arms tangled with one of his nieces between them, it took her a moment to regain her composure from the physical shock.

"Who's on the phone?" he asked, as if their proximity hadn't affected him at all. *Lucky.*

"Emily and Chase's lawyer."

"Swell…" After an awkward back and forth when neither could decide which way to go, he finally veered right. Seconds later, she heard him on the phone.

"Baxter. How have you been?"

Camille put her sleeping baby in her carrier alongside her sisters, then crept back to the kitchen.

"Sure," Jed said. "Monday at ten sounds fine."

More silence.

"Likewise. See you then." He hung up the phone before turning to the wall and resting his forehead against it.

"What's wrong?" she asked, fighting the urge to comfort him by running her hand up and down his back.

"Just more fun." His sarcasm rang through. Straightening, facing her, he rubbed his eyes with his thumb and forefinger. "Baxter informed me that my sister has a will. Since I'm apparently in it, he's stopping by for a visit on Monday."

"Think she named you the girls' guardian?"

He cupped both palms to his forehead. "Lord, I hope

not. I mean, like I was saying earlier, I love them, but I'm not wired for fatherhood."

"You've done a great job so far. In fact—" she cracked a grin "—the girls look better groomed than you. While they're sleeping, how about taking a shower? Meanwhile, I'll heat your dinner."

"Good call." Looking to his T-shirt's multiple stains, he nodded. "I've worn this for a couple of days."

"No judgment here."

"What do I do?"

"To take a shower? I don't understand."

He was back to cradling his forehead. "If Emily left me the kids. What do I do? It's not that the girls aren't great, but…" He released a long, slow stream of air, dropping his hands to slap them against his outer thighs. "After losing you. After what Alyssa did. I never planned on being a father. My only goal was to ride out my career until I'm an admiral or so old they force me into retirement."

"You can still do both of those things with daughters." She strove for a warm tone and hoped she met the mark. If he had been anyone but the first love she'd ever had and then lost, she'd have put her arms around him for the fiercest of hugs. But hugging him would be too hard. She could handle a lot, but not that. Holding him when she'd first learned of Emily's death had been painful enough. Not only had she lost her friend, but her ability to pretend Jed had ever fully been out of her life. Forgetting him had been an illusion she'd hidden behind a curtain in the deepest recesses of her mind. With the curtain drawn, she felt raw and exposed, and as if the only thing making her put one foot in front of the other was the fact that she and Jed were suddenly responsible for three helpless baby girls.

Only that wasn't entirely true, since she wasn't required to be here. Baxter hadn't mentioned Camille being in Emily's will.

At any time, she could walk away.

Probably *should* walk away.

But then she looked at Jed, his precious features pinched by grief, and what little humanity remained in her after the ugliness she'd witnessed back in Miami ached for him.

"Whatever you decide," she said, arms tingling from the effort of not reaching out to him, "I know you'll make the right decision. Monday is a day away. Tomorrow, let's try again to get the girls on a schedule, then we'll tackle Baxter's news when it comes. Sound like a plan?"

"Yeah…" His normally smooth voice rasped. Clearing his throat, he sharply looked away. "You always did have a knack for knowing just what to do." With a backhanded wave, he left the kitchen. Seconds later, she heard his footfalls on the stairs, presumably on the way to a shower.

He was right. She used to very much be a take-charge kind of woman. But that was before she'd accepted the job that destroyed all she used to be.

In this case, she wasn't sure what either of them should do. All she really knew was that for her love of Emily, Camille felt honor bound to watch over her daughters. Nothing else mattered—especially not her still chaotic feelings for their uncle.

Chapter 7

Jed blinked in his room's darkness, slow to wake.

Where am I?

Blaring from the baby monitor on his nightstand were the three tenors in their soprano glory.

He rubbed his eyes. "Coming…"

Sitting up, swinging his legs off the bed, his bare feet found the cold hardwood floor.

He took a quick pee, then half jogged to the nursery.

"I'm here," he said to Allie. "What's the problem?" The night-light provided enough of an ambient glow to not need the harsh overhead bulb.

He plucked her from her crib, patting her rump to find a full diaper.

Great.

He knew the drill and set about removing her old diaper, wiping her down, then wrapping her in a fresh one.

"Need help?"

A glance toward the door showed Camille leaning against the frame wearing an oversize Broncos T-shirt and nothing else.

Had her legs always been so long?

He gulped, refusing to allow his memory to travel back to times when it had been commonplace for him to run his hand along her inner thigh higher and higher, until she either laughingly screeched for him to stop or closed her eyes and gave her blessing for him to go further, carrying her higher without ever leaving who-ever's bed they happened to be sharing.

"Jed?"

He shook his head, then nodded. Help—yes.

"Mind fixing bottles?" he asked. With all three ba-bies now crying, they were probably hungry. "Or you can watch them while I make bottles? Either way, I'm guessing that's the only way we'll get more sleep."

"Agreed. Be right back."

Once she was gone, he held tight to the girls while positioning himself on the daybed Emily had placed against the windows overlooking the barn, so she and her babies could wave to Chase while he worked.

The screaming was taking a toll.

He breathed through rising panic. Why wouldn't they stop? What if they died, too? He knew the thought was ludicrous, but what were the odds of two healthy young adults passing within weeks of each other? He couldn't help having death on the brain.

Where was Camille?

As much as he hated to admit it, her mere pres-ence made him feel better. As if he just might make it through this nightmare until his mother found her way home.

His nieces kept crying and crying until the discordant notes made his ears ring and his teeth hurt. Jed tried jiggling and singing, but nothing worked.

Did he need to go get that SEAL survival manual and start reading again?

Finally, Camille was back. "Sorry it took so long. I had a devil of a time finding a can opener for the formula—which we're running low on." She handed him two bottles and kept one for herself, hefting Sallie into her arms before sitting beside him. "We'll need to head into town tomorrow for more."

He nodded.

With all three babies suckling, the silence struck him as sublime, yet his ears kept ringing.

"Good grief... That constant crying is tough."

"No kidding."

He repositioned Callie and Allie so he could sit in a more comfortable position. Too late he realized he might be more comfortable, but he'd also landed his thigh alongside Camille's. What was it about her thighs that he couldn't get enough of?

Too tired to move, he maintained his current position, but tried not to think about how good it would feel to again fall asleep against her.

Knowing he needed to get his mind off her soft, warm curves, he cleared his throat, then said, "Tell me about your job. Why you left. Last time my mom talked to yours, you were happy for the promotion."

"From the start I was in over my head—had no idea what I was getting into."

"Long hours? I can relate."

"Endless days never bothered me. The senseless violence did—especially against kids." She clutched Sallie closer, then squeezed her eyes shut. "Some of the things I saw…" She shuddered. "Stuff of nightmares. The monsters capable of such heinous acts couldn't have been human. It was too much. So I quit."

"But why'd you end up here? Why not transfer to a desk job?"

She shrugged. "I needed a clean slate. Once Mom told me Gramps wasn't doing so hot, I jumped at the chance to leave." Eyes open, she laughed. "Little did I know Mom conned me. Gramps doesn't need me any more than you do. But it makes me feel good to at least make sure he's eating regularly and taking his meds. He spends most of his time at the mine, leaving me with the *Young and the Restless* to keep me company."

"Still watching?" Every woman in his family and hers had been obsessed with the long-running soap for as long as he could remember.

"Every day. Don't even pretend you didn't watch, too, when you lived at home."

His lips curved into a smile. "Busted. Victor and Nikki still married?"

She laughed. "Married for the moment, but you know how that can change."

"Give it a month and their relationship is again doomed."

"Right."

The shared memory felt as good as having a companion to help him with this late-night feeding.

"Thanks again for hanging out with me," he said. "You're wrong about me not needing you. I thought I could tackle three babies on my own, but I was wrong."

"I doubt anyone could—even Emily."

"Wish I'd have done more for her—insisted she see a counselor."

"Did you have any idea how bad she was taking Chase's passing?"

He shook his head. "For me, she always put up a brave front. I'd catch her crying, but then she'd make up some excuse about her emotions being hormonal. I was so caught up in caring for these three—" he nodded to his now sleeping nieces "—that I never gave a thought to her being in real danger of... What? Losing her mind?"

"Don't say that." Camille stroked Sallie's hair. "I refuse to believe her death was anything but an accident. She needed to feel better and thought if one or two pills helped, three or four might work even better."

He snorted. "More like ten or twelve. Hell—maybe more."

"Regardless. Pain is pain. She needed it to stop and thought the medicine might help."

"So she did commit suicide?"

"Not intentionally." Camille kissed Sallie's forehead. "*Never* intentionally."

Nodding, with two babies in his arms, he had to wipe his silent tears by raising one shoulder at a time. He'd always hated crying. Viewed it as a sign of weakness. Lately, he couldn't seem to stop crying. Guess he had more in common with his nieces than he'd like to think.

She whispered, "We should put these little ladies back in their cribs and try getting at least a few more hours of rest for ourselves."

"Agreed."

"Stay put." She gingerly scooted off the daybed and

onto her feet. "Let me put Sallie in her crib, then I'll come back for the other two. I don't want to risk waking them with too much jostling."

"Valid point."

She soon had all three girls in their cribs and covered with fuzzy pink blankets.

He checked that the monitor's base station was still on, then they both crept from the room. After the door was safely closed, he exhaled. "We made it."

She held up her hand for a high five. "Teamwork makes the dream work."

He met her palm with his, but then opened his fingers, easing them between hers. "Thanks again. For everything."

"My pleasure," she said, with a faint smile and slight bow of her head. "You have no idea how good it feels to be needed." She maintained a surprisingly tight hold on his hand and he wasn't complaining. "Earlier? When we talked about my job. I think that was one of the toughest facts I had to face. I'd entered police work with the intention of making a difference. Cleaning up entire neighborhoods one street at a time. But the criminals and gangs and garden variety thugs—they're like a freaking game of Whac-A-Mole. We'd get a few behind bars, but more kept popping up. Far from making a difference, I was only placing myself on a hamster wheel, with no hope of ever catching up on my never-ending case log."

"Sorry." He stroked her palm with the pad of his thumb. "I truly am. I know after what happened to your father how much you wanted to make a difference."

"Right. Enough that I took a pass on what could have been the greatest thing to ever happen—marrying you."

What? Had she just admitted what he thought she had? That she regretted their breakup as much as he did?

"But that's water under both of our proverbial bridges," she continued. "All we can do now is plunge forward and try making the most of whatever time we have left."

"That's a fatalistic attitude. Do you think the middle of the night is the best time to be having this deep of a conversation?"

Shrugging, she yawned, covering her mouth with her free hand. "It's been bugging me for a while. No time like the present to get it out. If there's anything to be learned from Emily and Chase's passing, it's that there's no point in putting off what we can do or say today, because we may never see tomorrow. That message got slammed home for me dozens of times on the job. I'd show up to interview a witness, only to find him or her dead. It happened so often, I stopped being surprised. In fact, when I reached the point where I'd grown oblivious to the worst of the worst, that was when I knew it was time to pull the plug and get out while I still held a shred of humanity."

"I'm glad you did." On autopilot and too damned tired to think straight, he drew her into his arms for a proper hug. How was it that after all this time apart, holding her felt as if he'd finally found home? Just like they always had, her curves fitted perfectly against him.

"This is going to sound crazier than all of the rest of the crap I just spouted, but—"

"If that's how you feel, it's not crap," he said. "In fact, I wouldn't be surprised if you're suffering from a nasty case of PTSD. Happens all the time in my line of work. You should find yourself a good shrink."

"That's what my mom says. I went for a while on the department's dime, but she thinks I shouldn't have stopped."

"She's right."

There Camille went again with her smile. "I can't very well tell her that. I'd never hear the end of it."

"True." He couldn't help but smile back. "Sorry. Before I cut you off, you'd been about to say something crazy?"

"Yeah…" Keeping a tight hold on his hand, she flipped it over so that she tugged him along behind her while she aimed for her room. "Sleep with me."

"E-excuse me?"

"Get your mind out of the gutter. I'm talking strictly G-rated sleep. I don't want to be alone."

"I get it." He reluctantly released her hand. "Let me grab the other half of the monitor from my room, and I'll meet you in bed."

"Awesome. Thanks."

He should be the one thanking her.

Ten minutes later, as Jed spooned her with his hand resting on her belly, overwhelming gratitude threatened to once again bring him to tears. But this time, he held it together.

He'd take the chance to find comfort together, which they both desperately needed. Just two long-time friends indulging in a sleepover.

The thing was, back when they'd been kids, he hadn't been hyperaware of the tops of his fingers being perilously near the bottoms of her full breasts…

What they currently shared was no big deal, right?

Camille woke with her T-shirt midway up her back and her ass pressed against Jed's morning wood. How easy it would be to turn over, climb atop him and ride her way into a fantastic day.

Sounded like a solid plan until she heard a whimper on the baby monitor. Seconds later came another, and another, until all three girls wailed.

"Please make it stop," her companion mumbled against her back. His breath warmed the sensitive spot at the base of her neck.

She squeezed her thighs together extra tightly, trying to make her longing for him go away. It did not.

Neither did the crying.

"Are we ever going to catch a break?" he asked, already rolling away from her and off the bed.

"Afraid not…" Camille also reluctantly left the cozy bed. She hadn't slept so soundly in years. Did she have Jed to thank? Probably. Not a good thing, but she wouldn't have time to dwell on the ramifications until later—if ever.

On their second full day of caring for the triplets, Camille and Jed had already established somewhat of a routine. They formed a diaper-changing assembly line, then carted everyone to the kitchen, where Camille prepped bottles and Jed juggled the threesome on his lap in the comfy U-shaped booth Chase had built when he and Emily refurbished the kitchen in anticipation of their growing family.

With everyone fed and burped, but still awake, she and Jed plopped them into their trio of wind-up swings.

"Whew…" He ran his hand over his stubble. "It's good to have a breather."

"Amen." She joined him in the booth with a steaming cup of coffee and a box of graham crackers. "Not the most nutritious breakfast, but better than nothing."

"Thanks." He crunched his way through a six-stack of crackers. "I've had way worse."

"Name it."

"Worms, maggots, grass, dandelions, rat…need me to go on?"

She blanched. "I get the picture. As bad as my job got, at least I was never far from a 7-Eleven."

"That's a serious blessing."

Grinning, she shook her head. "Last night I couldn't sleep, so—"

"Wait—when I was with you, I for sure heard snoring in under a minute of your head hitting the pillow."

Cheeks blazing, she said, "I meant before then."

"Okay. Proceed…"

His smile had her smiling again. "While I was awake, I researched a few sites on establishing newborn sleep schedules. How old are the girls?"

"Ten weeks? Maybe a little older? I was overseas when they were born."

Camille took her phone from her back pocket, pulling up the page. "Since the girls have never really had stability, I propose we start them on a four-week-old routine. They've been eating roughly every four hours, so we're actually lucky. Average is two to three hours."

"At that rate, we'd literally do nothing but feed, burp, change diapers, rinse and repeat."

"Exactly. Take a look at this schedule I screenshot." She passed him her phone, which held a photo from amotherfarfromhome.com:

7:30-8:00 am—wake up and feed
8:30 am—down for a nap
10:30 am—feed, change diaper, play

11:10 am—down for a nap
1:00 pm—feed, change diaper, play
1:40 pm—down for a nap
3:30 pm—feed, change diaper, play
4:10 pm—down for a nap
6:00 pm—feed, change diaper, play, bath
6:30 pm—down for a catnap
7:30-8:00 pm—change diaper, put to bed for the
night

"Seriously?" Jed took a long time reading before returning her phone. "I've launched invasions with more wiggle room."

"That may well be, but if we ever want to sleep till the girls enter kindergarten, this is what we're facing."

"Kindergarten, huh?" With hands steepled, he stared out the nearest window at the horses grazing in their favorite field. The pastoral scene should have made him smile. Instead, it reminded him he still had the horses, chickens and goats to feed. Before tragedy struck, how in the hell had Chase and Emily so cheerfully tackled their lives? "I can't see either of us sticking around that long."

"Granted. I'm just saying..."

"I get it."

Camille looked to the girls, who were sharing a rare adorable moment of in-unison staring at their hot pink socks while the swings carried them back and forth. The thought of leaving them made her melancholy, but she'd known from the start this was a temporary gig. All she'd ever wanted was to help people. To make a difference. She'd proved an epic failure at her career—no. That wasn't entirely true. She had helped solve many cases, but not enough. Never enough. And no matter how many monsters she'd helped put behind bars, more always emerged from dark corners. Regardless of how brief a time she had with the girls, she vowed to do her best to keep them fed, clean and happy—at least as happy as they could be having lost both parents. "I, um, also did some reading on whether or not babies mourn. Turns out they do, which might be why they've been crying so much."

"Makes sense. What can we do to help?"

"Hold them and love them. Make sure they know someone will always be there for them."

"But I won't. Wish I could always be there for them, but eventually, I'll have to return to base. You eventually need to stop hiding from whatever went down in Miami and rejoin adult society."

"Is that what you think I'm doing?" Her chest tightened. Fists clenched, for the girls' sake she managed not to raise her voice. *"Hiding?"*

"Aren't you? I don't mean it as an insult. Just stating a fact."

"Screw you." She took her empty mug to the porcelain sink.

"Hey…" He was suddenly behind her, and she regrettably felt his radiant heat. When he cupped his hands around her shoulders, spinning her to face him, she pressed her lips tight. "Sorry if I hit a nerve. It's okay—I mean, if you never choose to go back to your detective gig."

"It wasn't a *gig*, but what I believed to be my life's calling. There's a massive difference. How would you like it if I said Navy SEALs are nothing more than a glorified scout group for grown-ups?"

Chapter 8

"Ouch."

"Exactly." Camille wrenched free from Jed's hold. This close, she couldn't think. Breathe. She was good and mad at him and intended to stay that way.

"I said I'm sorry." He raised his hands as if reaching out to her, but then lowered them. "My career means everything to me. I can't imagine walking away."

"I didn't just walk away, but... Never mind, you wouldn't understand."

"Try me."

"Have you ever seen the aftermath of a parent trying to dispose of the baby boy he's just killed while on a bath salts rampage?"

"Lord..." He crossed the room to her, pulling her hard against him. To her surprise, she let him. Whether sensing the change in mood or just plain missing their mom and dad, the girls whimpered and fussed before launching into full-blown cries. "Can they not?"

"It's okay." She extracted herself from his hold. "Caring for them helps shift my focus from dead babies to living."

It took an hour to get the girls to stop crying.

During that time, Camille realized that in a sense, Jed had been right about her walking away. That had been exactly what she'd done—more like ran. And that should have been okay. Leaving had been her choice. But as snippy and raw as the topic made her, clearly, she still wasn't feeling all that great about the decision.

She and Jed shared the den sofa.

His eyes were closed, but she couldn't tell if he was sleeping.

The girls had finally crashed on the quilts near the crackling fire.

"Where are we on the schedule?" Jed asked.

A strangled laugh escaped her. "What schedule?"

"We still need to go to the store?"

"'Fraid so."

"Should we go ahead and get it over with?"

"I guess." It didn't matter that she'd gotten plenty of rest during the night's second half. Exhaustion now claimed her, making her ache as if she'd caught a nasty flu.

It took an hour's worth of back-and-forthing to load fully equipped diaper bags, the supersized stroller and three babies into Emily's SUV.

Plus, Jed had to check all the livestock's feed and water.

Once they were finally underway, with Jed behind the wheel, the crew was back at it again with the screaming. Once-sunny skies had turned overcast and a cold wind was strong enough to buffet even the large vehicle.

"Thought babies loved car rides?" Jed asked.

"Me, too," she said. "Or is it an urban myth?"

"Could be. Should we play some music?"

"Like nursery rhymes? Pop? Country?" Emily had left a USB cord plugged into the car's stereo. Camille used it to connect her phone. "Unfortunately, since I have no signal, our only options are what I've got downloaded on iTunes."

"Just keep playing till we find something that works."

Adele—nope.

Lady Gaga—if possible, the girls screamed louder.

Yahtzee! George Strait's "Amarillo by Morning" soothed them like magic baby elixir.

"Put that song on auto-repeat," Jed said.

Camille did. And the three-minute song played fifteen times before Jed pulled into an isolated space at King Sooper's supermarket.

Sadly, by the time they'd wrestled all three infants from their safety seats and into the stroller-for-three, they were all crying again.

Did they dislike cold wind as much as she did?

"Look." Jed worked his head from side to side. Kink in his neck? "I seriously don't mean this to sound like a man-versus-woman thing, but since you seem to know more about what the girls need as far as formula and diapers, how about I stay in the car with them and George Strait? You do the shopping, then I'll unload and put it all away. Sound like a plan?"

"I like it," she said.

He handed over his Visa card.

"I can buy it." She struggled to keep her hair from her eyes in the wild wind.

"They're my nieces. Please, let me."

She pocketed his card. "Anything you especially need?"

"More sandwich fixings. Coke. Am I allowed to have beer?"

"I don't know why not. I mean, I don't think you should get hammered, but one or two wouldn't hurt. It's not like you're breast-feeding. I know I'm grabbing a bottle of merlot."

"Great. Coors. Cheetos." He'd already started putting their charges back in the car. "Chocolate chip cookies—I'm in need of serious comfort food."

"Would you be amenable to me cooking something a little more wholesome than stuff from a package?"

"What do you have in mind?" He made a sour face. "I don't do tofu or hummus or any of that yoga health-nut stuff."

"Yessir," she said, with a mock salute in deference to his military, he-man tone. "I was thinking meat loaf and roasted chicken. Banana bread and oatmeal cookies—those sorts of things."

He tipped his head back and groaned. "Woman, are you trying to feed me or seduce me?"

Both? There went her stupid overheating cheeks. She ducked to avoid him seeing just how much his offhand comment affected her. "My primary goal is to keep you healthy until your mom gets home. I can't have you caring for the girls and animals on a diet of beer and Cheetos."

He winked. "You'd be amazed how great I perform on that combo."

Shaking her head and laughing, she delivered a back-handed wave before leaving him and entering the store.

Nearly four hundred dollars and a heaping cart later, Camille exited to find Jed asleep at the wheel. The SUV's engine idled and a muted George Strait was still crooning.

She cupped her hands around her eyes, peering into the tinted backseat window. All three girls were wide-awake and gumming their fists, or fingers, or in Sallie's case, the hot pink sock that she'd somehow managed to remove from her right foot.

Camille hated waking Jed, but when she tried opening the rear hatchback, she found it locked.

Leaving the cart, she walked around to the vehicle's front to knock on the driver's side window.

Jed woke with a start, accidentally conking his elbow against the horn.

Cue terrified screams of the variety even George Strait couldn't soothe.

"Sorry," Camille said, when Jed climbed out of the car.

"It's whatever. See what you can do to get them under control. I'll tackle the groceries."

"Thanks."

She was in the rear with the girls when he asked, "Where's the cart?"

"What do you mean?" she asked over the seat back.

"I mean, there are no groceries back here."

"I left the cart right where you're standing."

He looked left and right, then groaned.

"What's wrong?"

"Look! Is that it?" He pointed to the far side of the

parking lot where the wind had caught their overloaded cart, sailing it perilously close to the edge of a deep ravine.

"Yes! *Run!*"

Jed hauled ass after the rogue cart, snagging it by the handle mere seconds before losing dozens of sacks filled with food and baby necessities to a ravine with walls too steep to climb without ropes.

At the rocky bottom roared a swift-running stream.

The remains of three rusty carts rested on their sides alongside assorted beer cans, bottles and other trash.

The wind filled a plastic sack, transforming it into a balloon floating high above Jed's head.

Raising his coat collar against the falling temperature, he rolled the cart back to the SUV, to find his nieces blessedly quiet and Camille…laughing?

"What's so funny?" he asked through the open hatch while placing a five-pound sack of potatoes against the wheel well.

"The sight of you chasing down our runaway cart. I had no idea you could run so fast."

He grinned and winked. "I had no idea you weren't smart enough to hold on to a shopping cart in forty-knot gusts."

Kneeling in her seat, hugging the headrest while supervising his work, she stuck out her tongue.

"Since when did you get so sassy?" *And sexy?* The things he wouldn't mind doing to tame her, if they didn't have three tiny chaperones sharing the car… Her cheeks were flushed from the cold, her hazel eyes bright. Her long hair all wind-tousled and wild.

It irked him to no end that she used to be his and now…

They were virtual strangers.

He finished loading, parked the cart in its designated corral, then hopped back behind the wheel.

"Sorry I laughed. I just couldn't believe that after all we'd already been through, you were now having to chase a runaway shopping cart. It struck me as kooky enough to be funny."

"*Kooky?* You use that kind of language around the hard-boiled detectives you used to work with?"

Her smile faded. A shadow passed over her expression, darkening it just like the now angry sky.

"I didn't mean anything by that," he said.

"No. For the record, I never used words like that." She'd straightened in her seat, looking away from him to fasten her seat belt. "Interesting how when my vocabulary largely consisted of pint-sized body bags and blood coagulation times, that didn't leave a whole lot of room for *kooky*."

"I get that. Sorry."

"I just find it tough to joke about my work."

"Is that what you think I'm doing?"

"Sure feels like it." She fumbled with the heater controls until a warm stream left the vents.

"Accept my apology or don't. Honestly? It's been a damn long time since I've been around a woman and I'm rough around the edges. Toss in constant sleep deprivation and I'm not exactly up to speed on my social graces."

"Still…"

"It's all I've got." Sighing, he slouched in his seat. "I'm sick of bickering. You didn't used to be so touchy. We always bantered back and forth and you gave as good as you got."

"What if I can't? What if the part of me capable of firing back those zingers carefully targeted to put you in your place no longer works?" Silvery tears trailed down her cheeks. Her motions almost vicious, as if she resented her body showing weakness, she swiped them away.

"Babe…" Unable to stop himself, he reached out to her, cupping his hand to her cheek, brushing more tears with the pad of his thumb.

She started to push him away, but then leaned into him, covering his hand with hers.

Staring straight ahead, she said, "You were right about me running. Hiding. This place—your farm and Gramps's. This town. They feel safe. There are no gang members shooting each other for no better reason than they got caught standing on the wrong side of the street. Back in Miami, I was always afraid. Waking up with night sweats from horrifying dreams. I begged Mom to move, but she insists her neighborhood is safe. But as a soldier, tell me, Jed, is anywhere on this earth truly safe?"

Sighing, he smoothed her hair back from her forehead. "Let's just say there are degrees of safety. You're right that, in terms of not getting shot, our mountain is a good place to be. But that doesn't mean there aren't hunting accidents and hikers dying from exposure, and cars and grocery carts careening over cliffs."

"Grocery carts?" Her smile didn't reach her eyes, but it was a start toward lightening the heavy mood.

"None of us can hope for total control. At best, all we can do is hedge our bets and pray for the best."

Sniffling, she nodded. "What's wrong with us? Neither of us used to be this emotional."

"That was before two close relations younger than us died within weeks of each other. Whether we want to accept it or not, it takes a toll."

"You're right." She fished through the glove box for a napkin and found one, which she used to blow her nose. "Ready to head home?"

Home. Such a funny word. Not ha-ha funny, but odd.

The old farm hadn't been home to him in over a decade, but now—with Camille—it had become the one place he most wanted and needed to be.

One of the babies fussed, which in turn activated her sisters.

Jed backed the vehicle out of its spot. "Mind putting George back on? I'm afraid without him it may be a very long trip."

His heart skipped at the sight of Camille's sideways smile. "Remind me to write him a thank-you note."

Back at the house, while Jed hauled groceries, Camille tackled the babies. They needed diapers changed and feeding.

Since Jed was in and out of the kitchen, she took the girls upstairs one at a time for diaper duty, then popped them back in their carriers.

Next, while Jed stowed groceries in cupboards and the pantry, she set the babies in a row, made their bottles, then formed an assembly line for feeding. Since she could hold only two bottles at a time, she propped Callie's bottle with a rolled dishrag.

"I applaud your ingenuity." Jed set the last few bags on the counter. "What I'm not a fan of is how much stuff you bought, because I'm too exhausted to haul it. You must really love to cook."

"I do." She used a burp cloth to wipe formula from Allie's chin. "Hope you like to eat?"

"Yes, ma'am."

"Is it still blustery outside?"

"The wind's not as strong up here. Why?"

"I'd love to stretch my legs. Should we bundle up the girls and introduce them to Lucy and Ethel?"

"If you want." He stood with his back to her, arranging canned goods with precision and order. He stretched to put a cracker box on a shelf above his head. The pose showed off his muscles to a ridiculous degree. It wasn't fair that after all this time, he looked better than he had before.

When he turned, she glanced away, not wanting him to catch her staring.

"It's okay, you know."

"What?" She focused on wiping the sides of Callie's mouth, since she'd finished her bottle.

"Admiring the view..." He laughed.

"You wish." She pitched the burp cloth at him.

Funny how they'd slipped back into old patterns. One of the things she'd enjoyed most about them as a couple was how they could transition from a serious topic to lighthearted and back as easily as flipping mood switches.

"Holler when you're ready to head outside."

"I'm good now."

"Let me take the stroller from the SUV and I'll meet you out front."

"I'll get coats, hats and mittens."

As was starting to be the norm, it took forever to get everyone dressed and ready for their outing. But once she stood in the pasture alongside the horses Emily and

Chase had loved, Camille breathed deeply of the chilly air, which smelled musky and loamy with spring.

She spied lavender-toned wild crocus, plucking a few to later put in a vase on the windowsill above the kitchen sink.

"Hey, ladies…" While Jed steered the all-terrain stroller across the short grass, Camille set the flowers safely atop the stroller canopy before rubbing the horses' noses.

Their snorts wreathed their heads in foggy exhalations.

The babies stared in wonder.

"I worried they might be scared, but more than anything they seem fascinated," Camille said.

"Good." He stroked Lucy's cheek. "Emily always loved horses. For Christmas, Mom and Dad got her horse toys or earrings or T-shirts—at least until she got Lucy for her sixteenth birthday." His eyes welled up. "I think the only day I ever saw her happier was when she married Chase. I couldn't be here with her when she had the girls."

Crushing sadness threatened to steal the air from her lungs. "I didn't realize she'd had Lucy so long? Geez, even the horse must be in mourning."

"Wouldn't surprise me. Chase bought her Ethel as an engagement gift. They used to go on overnight trail rides. Mom would get all bent out of shape about it not being proper, but then Dad would remind her that since she planned on marrying the guy, it wasn't as if they didn't already know about the birds and bees." He laughed. "You and I sure did."

"Jed!" She smacked his arm, but the soft pink

woolen mittens she'd borrowed from the coat closet didn't deliver much of a punch.

"It's the truth."

There went her cheeks again, blazing with enough heat that she took off her scarf and fanned herself with it.

Golden afternoon sun punched through the clouds, accompanying them while they crossed the pasture in companionable silence. Jed still pushed the stroller, while Camille stayed in line with the horses, which seemed appreciative of the attention.

She'd forgotten how pretty the farm was, nestled in an alpine meadow, surrounded on three sides by pine forests and snow-capped peaks. The winters were long, but the summers were sublime. Some of the happiest times of her life had been spent in this very field.

As kids, they'd played tag, hide-and-seek, and built forts from fallen branches in the warm months and from snow during the cold.

Once she'd been old enough to appreciate Jed for more than just being Emily's fun big brother, they'd played games of an entirely different kind. Truth or dare. Spin the bottle. Strip poker.

This used to be her happy place, but with Emily and Chase gone, all she now associated with the farm was tragedy.

"Guess we've shot your fancy new schedule all to hell?" Jed stopped at the tree line to stretch.

"It's okay. With this rowdy bunch, maybe it's best if we fly by the seat of our pants?"

Cringing, he said, "In most matters, I do love a good plan."

"Me, too. But I'm afraid this is a case of the inmates running the asylum."

Laughing, he said, "You're probably right. Speaking of running things, what are you making for dinner? And do we need to take something down to your grandpa?"

A wave of guilt surged through her. "I'm a terrible person. I haven't even thought about him all day."

"Don't be so hard on yourself. Truth be told, judging by what you've said about your gramps spending so much time up at that old mine, he probably hasn't thought much about you, either."

"Thanks?" Counsel like that made her think she'd have been better off leaving Jed at the house and keeping the horses for company.

"You know what I mean." He turned the stroller around. "Since the sun's setting, let's get you and the kiddos inside, then I need to circle back to the barn. I'd like Lucy and Ethel inside for the night, plus I'll make sure the chickens and goats have their heating lamps on."

"What if I'd rather do all of that and you tackle the babies?"

"Fine—assuming you don't mind having tuna straight from the can for dinner, with a few dozen shakes of Tabasco."

"You're just saying that to get out of diaper duty."

He winked. "Guess there's only one way to find out."

"Whatever." They finished the trek back in silence. At the pasture gate, she hugged both horses' necks, promising to visit again soon.

A quick diaper check found everyone surprisingly dry. Since no one was crying, Camille settled the girls into their swings while she made a dinner of meat loaf, scalloped potatoes and salad.

Jed came in from the barn and washed up at the

kitchen sink. "Smells heavenly in here. Thanks for cooking."

"You're welcome. Guess while everyone's calm I need to take Gramps his supper."

"Want me to take it for you? Or we all go together?"

"Thanks, but no." *I need a breather from not just your nieces, but you.* "I won't be long."

"I've got an idea." Darting in front of her, blocking the kitchen pass-through, he said, "What if your grandfather came here to live till Mom gets home? There are plenty of rooms."

"Seriously?"

"Why not? The more the merrier."

She had no answer for him—at least not one she cared to share. The more time they spent together, the more they were starting to feel like a family. Not a good thing, considering he was leaving for California as soon as his mom returned, and Camille had witnessed too much pain to ever expose herself to that kind of emotional liability.

Being a parent meant opening her heart, but how could she do that when she feared it was permanently closed?

She forced her way around him, trying but failing to ignore icy-hot tingles of awareness stemming from their merest touch. There'd once been a time when she might have considered that fact significant. Like it meant she and Jed were destined to be together. But that was as foolish as believing there would ever again be peace and contentment in her world.

Chapter 9

"Think that's funny?" Jed scooped a handful of no-tear bubbles onto Callie's head. He leaned farther over the edge of the tub, trying to get all three tenors scrubbed and rinsed before Camille got home.

There was that word again. *Home*. He'd never tell her, but without her here, the place felt lonely. He felt lonely but fought the feeling by horsing around more with his nieces. If they had to have bath time, might as well make it fun.

He crowned all three babies with bubbles, giving them views of each other by rearranging their low-slung infant bath seats.

Sallie and Allie couldn't stop grinning at the sight.

Callie cooed and slapped her palms against the warm water.

"I didn't know you were developmentally able to

smile," he said, truly awed at the cuteness, "but I'm not complaining."

Jed indulged in playtime for a few more minutes, then got back to business, washing the girls with mild soap and a bath mitt, then rinsing with a plastic cup.

He drained the tub but was unsure how to dress and dry everyone at the same time, when all three shivered from the shift from warm water to chilly night air. The old house was drafty. If Jed was sticking around, he'd need to look into adding more insulation. But with him soon returning to base, he'd hire a contractor to tackle the job.

He wrapped the babies in their zoo-themed hooded towels. Allie was a lion. Callie a giraffe. And Sallie, a hippo.

"You all look very ferocious," Jed said, along with a teasing animal roar.

The trio didn't look amused.

"You gals are no fun."

To prove it, they started to cry.

"Aw, come on. We were having fun."

They cried louder.

Jed's night went downhill from there.

Would Camille ever return?

He dried his nieces' tiny limbs, lotioned them, diapered and dressed them. Still they cried.

Since they were still small enough for him to carry all three at once, he scooped them from Allie's crib, where he'd corralled them after cleaning the mess bathing had created, then hauled them to the kitchen, being careful to support their heads against his chest.

Once there, he realized he'd left their carriers upstairs.

By now, the trio had worked up a helluva tantrum. He didn't know if they were hungry, missing their mom and dad or just pissed at their tiny corner of the world. Whatever the problem, he didn't have a clue how to solve it.

His only option was to triage the situation, breaking it down one emergency at a time. Most pressing, setting the girls in a safe place.

He eyed the colorful rag rug in the center of the kitchen floor and knelt, depositing the girls in a howling, red-faced jumble at his feet.

Time to work the next problem—making bottles. Having Camille fix them had been a luxury he now missed. He knew how to do it, but that didn't mean he liked it. More and more he needed her, and he wasn't too proud to admit it.

The girls might not be happy, but they were safe—for the moment, all that mattered. Their fury struck a chord in him he'd never before seen and didn't like.

He felt panicked and frenzied, desperate to calm and soothe them.

He'd spent a decade learning to maintain his composure no matter how chaotic a situation. But no amount of training could have prepared him for this.

Hunched over, he forced deep, slow breaths. He needed to center himself. Get his head back in the game. His nieces were expressing themselves the only way they knew how. Their tantrum wasn't personal. Just a form of communication that Jed had never before encountered.

Like the first time he'd heard Farsi.

One last exhale and he was good to go, opening formula and fitting the bottles with plastic liners, filling them with liquid, then screwing on the lids.

"All right, crew…" He joined them on the floor. "Since I'm not sure what else to do with you, let's get you fed right here and now."

At first, they were too frenzied to suckle, but eventually they calmed enough to focus, and then finish their meals.

Jed glanced at his hands supporting three bottles to find himself trembling. What the hell?

SEALs don't succumb to bouts of nerves.

He heard the front door open and close.

"Cam?"

"Yep! Sorry it took me so long. Gramps lost his—" She froze in the kitchen pass-through. "Why are you all on the floor?"

"Turns out I owe every mother on the planet a massive apology. Caring for one baby is no joke—three? They've been crying and crying, and I felt like I was losing my mind."

"Aw…" She set her purse and an overnight bag on the kitchen table, kicked off her purple Uggs and joined them on the rug. "What happened?"

"I lost my mind."

"Understandable. Why do you think I left?" She elbowed him.

"Yeah, well, tomorrow I'm taking your grandfather out to eat. Maybe to one of those swanky steak houses in Aspen?"

"Keep dreaming…"

"I don't get a night off?"

"Nope. But you are welcome to a break. Go watch a ball game or mess around online. Since you've already got everyone in pj's and they look squeaky clean, I'm assuming you gave them a bath?"

"Affirmative. That part wasn't too bad, but things went downhill quick after that."

"What happened?" She drew Allie onto her lap for a cuddle. The other girls still hadn't finished their bottles.

"No clue. One minute they were fine—even smiling over the bath bubbles—then they freaked. I'm not sure if I did something wrong or—"

"Stop. Remember that they're reacting to changes around them they don't understand."

"That makes sense, but what can we do?"

"I did some more research while waiting for Gramps to safely get out of the shower so he wouldn't break a hip. Is there anything left around here that might still smell like Emily?" Kissing the crown of the baby's head, she added, "Maybe her pillow? A sweater?"

"Let's check her room. I'm sure there's a lot of stuff."

It took a few more minutes for the other two girls to finish. Since both of his charges seemed content on the floor, he left the bottles beside them, then stood. "Help?" Having set the baby she was holding alongside her sisters, Camille held up her hands. He instead grasped her under her arm, hefting her in one fluid motion onto her feet. "Whoa…" Laughing, she clutched his chest to steady herself. "That was like an amusement park ride."

"Never let it be said I'm not a great ride."

Camille rolled her eyes.

They plucked the babies up and carried them to Emily and Chase's room. Since Camille was the only one with a free hand, she opened the closed door on the dark space, feeling as if she were stepping into a tomb.

"I can't do this." Jed stood frozen in the hall. The only light came from a lamp that had a fiberglass trout for a base. "No way I can go in her room. It's too soon."

"No worries. Come on." Temporarily abandoning her mission, Camille led the way to the nursery, where he started placing the two babies he held in their separate cribs. But she stopped him with her hand on his forearm. "For tonight, let's experiment with them sleeping together."

"Isn't that dangerous?"

"Not from what I've read. It's comforting. Think about it. They've been crammed in your sister's belly for nine months. Why would they want to be separated now?"

"Makes sense." He set Callie and Sallie in Allie's crib.

Camille added Allie. "Hang tight. I'm going to get Chase and Emily's blanket."

"Thanks."

She again had her hand on his arm, this time giving him a light squeeze—just enough to let him know she cared. The gesture felt not only good, but natural. Camille was done pretending they were strangers, when nothing could be further from the truth. They might never again be a couple, but she needed him as a friend.

Back to the master bedroom. Camille paused just outside the door for a nice deep breath. At the time she'd suggested it, this had seemed like a good idea. Now, she wasn't so sure. It somehow felt wrong to riffle through the deceased couple's things.

Even though it's for the best cause?

Camille put aside her doubts in favor of flipping on the overhead light, then making a beeline for the double bed. It was unmade—not at all like Emily, who'd kept a tidy home. The messy bed spoke volumes on how overwhelmed the young widow must have been feeling.

"I'm sorry," Camille whispered to the smiling photo of Emily and Chase sitting atop the dresser. It somehow felt sacrilegious to speak out loud. "I should have been here for you. Instead, I was too wrapped up in my own issues—none of which compare to what you must have been going through."

The squeezing pain in her chest returned, along with a knot in her throat.

Grab the blanket and get out of here, her conscious mind coaxed.

Not only did Jed and the babies need her, but she needed them. She'd never expected how good it would feel once again being part of a team—however dysfunctional.

Camille made quick work of removing the blanket, then held it to her face, dragging in a deep, shuddering inhalation of the scent of her dear, lifelong friend. Faint roses from her favorite soap she'd always bought at the local farmers' market. A hint of lemon from the homemade lotion she picked up at the same stall.

If Camille recognized Emily's precious essence, surely her girls would, too? But if they did, would it confuse them all the more? She wanted the blanket to be a comfort, but what if it made them hurt worse?

She hesitated. "Em? Chase? If you can hear me, what do you think? Am I making the right choice?"

A low rumble erupted from the wall behind her, nearly making Camille leap out of her skin. But then she clutched the blanket closer, laughing at herself, realizing the sound had been the old central heat unit lumbering on.

A sign from beyond? Probably not.

But maybe.

After carrying the blanket out into the hall, she closed the master bedroom door behind her.

In the nursery, she found the babies still fussy and Jed lying on the floor in front of Allie's crib, eyes closed, with his arms crossed over his head. "I'm officially crying uncle," he said. "I can do that, right? Since I am their uncle?"

"I suppose…" Camille would have laughed if his defeated tone hadn't sounded so sad. "I found Emily's favorite blanket and it does smell like her. I'm not sure if this will work, but…" She draped it over the cranky triplets. "I guess at this point anything's worth a try."

Jed left the floor to join her at the crib's edge.

At first, nothing happened, but then Allie fisted the soft fabric, drawing it toward her. Her sisters followed suit.

"I'll be damned…" Jed murmured under his breath. "They really are missing her."

"I know I am."

"Me, too." He shocked her by draping his arm across her shoulders. There was nothing romantic about the casual gesture, so why did her every nerve ending feel on high alert? "I appreciate you coming up with this plan. Good call."

Hardly in the mood to celebrate, she slipped her arm around his waist, resting her head on his shoulder. "What should we do with this sudden bonus time without screaming babies?"

He rested his head against hers. "What if I told you the only thing I really want to do is sleep?"

"I'd say that sounds like an awesome plan."

Jed woke Monday morning with a knot in his stomach the size of a battleship.

With Baxter expected around ten, he took Camille up on her offer to watch the girls while he tended to the animals.

The day was sunny, but still colder than he'd like for spring. A light breeze blew out of the north, making him wonder if another wintry surprise was on the way.

"Good morning, ladies," he said to Lucy and Ethel, while breaking the thin layer of ice on their water trough.

They snorted, but otherwise seemed disinterested, preferring to continue grazing on the new shoots of emerald green forcing up through the otherwise brown earth.

"You ladies do know that aside from the rooster, I'm the only man around?"

Apparently unimpressed, they didn't even look up.

After breaking a fresh hay bale for them, he moved on to the goats, which were their usual rowdy but friendly selves.

The chickens seemed subdued from the morning chill, but their heat lamp had the coop toasty and he collected a dozen eggs in the basket Camille had given him for the task. Wonder if she knew the recipe for her mother's deviled eggs?

"How was everyone?" she asked, when he entered the kitchen through the back door. She stood at the sink, washing breakfast dishes.

The babies cooed in their swings.

"Good. Though Lucy and Ethel were playing hard to get."

"Did they catch wind of your ladies' man reputation?"

"Ha-ha." He removed the thick Cargill jacket he'd borrowed from Chase, hanging it on the hook by the door. His cowboy boots were next to go, and then the battered brown cowboy hat his dad had given him ages ago was last to be hung, on the doorknob.

"How are you feeling about Baxter's visit?" she asked. "He should be here any time."

"Thanks for reminding me." He opened the fridge and removed a Coke. "Is it too early for a beer?"

"Probably, but if you want one, I've got breath mints in my purse."

"I knew there was a reason I liked you."

She reset the timers on all three swings, poured herself a fresh coffee, then sat at the booth with a magazine he knew she'd picked up at the grocery store and had been trying to read ever since.

"Seriously, though…" He sat across from her. "While I was outside, I gave a lot of thought to what I'm going to say if he tells me Emily wanted me to assume responsibility for the girls."

"And?"

"And…" He took a long swig of his soda, pretending it was something stronger. "I'll tell him no. Not only do I still have a couple years left on my commission, but I'm not cut out to be a dad. I think I must lack some basic caring gene?"

"I doubt that. From what I've seen, you're great with the girls."

He rested his head on the table. "But is going through the motions the same as being a good parent? I mean—"

The landline's shrill ring caught them both off guard.

They looked to the babies, but fortunately for their sanity, the trio loved their swings and didn't seem to notice the noise.

Jed answered before the third ring, fearing another call from the lawyer, possibly to reschedule. "Hello?"

"Jed?" His knees turned to rubber. He braced his hands against the wall.

"Mom? Where are you?" Lord… Just hearing her familiar voice returned him to childhood, when she'd made everything okay with a Spiderman Band-Aid, a hug or a cookie. "Are you almost home?"

"Afraid not," she said through the crackling connection. "My satellite phone had an unfortunate accident with a goat, and I don't expect transport out of the region for at least another week—possibly two. How are you holding up?"

"I'm okay," he lied.

"I still can't believe your sister's gone. I feel like I've been sleepwalking since hearing the news—trying everything I can to get back, but fate keeps conspiring against me."

"The girls are taking it hard. They cry incessantly."

"Poor things."

"Last night, Camille had the bright idea to—"

"She's still there? Helping you?"

"Yes. She's been great."

"I can't tell you how much better that makes me feel. You always seemed happier with her in your life."

"It's not like that—we're not together. I'm due back on base as soon as you get home."

"That may be, but—" The connection turned to nothing but static, and then dead air. *Shit*.

He slapped his palm against the wall. "Lost her."

"Maybe she'll call again?"

"Doubtful."

She'd left the booth and her magazine to place her hand on his back. "Sorry. Did she say when she'll be home?"

"A week or two. But her team visits villages so remote I'm surprised she was even able to get a second call out."

"Before you know it, she'll be home and all of this will be behind you."

He nodded.

The doorbell rang.

"I'll get it," he said, thankful the babies' calm streak still held.

"Want to talk with him in here or in the den?"

"Here. I want you with me." Whatever his sister had to say from beyond the grave, he didn't especially want to know. Sounded selfish of him, and he was sure it was, but the pain of losing her was still too fresh and raw. He was still too pissed at her. Accident or not, what had she been thinking? Oh yeah—she hadn't been thinking at all about the three babies she'd left behind.

Jed stormed to the door, dreading the lawyer's news.

"Hello, Jed," Baxter said. "Long time, no see." The potbellied, balding man held out his gloved hand for Jed to shake.

"Wish we were meeting under different circumstances." Jed stepped back, gesturing him into the house. "Last time I saw you was, what? Chase and Em's wedding?"

"I believe so. Sadly, I was out of town for your father's funeral."

"Too damn many funerals," Jed muttered under his breath.

"I couldn't agree more."

"Let me take your coat and gloves." Camille entered from the kitchen. "Good to see you again. How's your wife? Helena, right?"

"Yes. Thank you, she's well. Wrapped up in the new theater group that's formed in town. Some Hollywood bigwig bought a place just west of here and last year he donated a community center and little theater. It's been a boost to local morale—especially during the winter."

"I'll bet."

Baxter held out his briefcase. "Where should we sit? I do have several documents for you, Jed, to sign."

"Kitchen table's fine." He led the way.

"Aren't you little angels," Baxter said on his way past the babies.

"They're being shockingly well-behaved," Camille said. "Trust me, we're on borrowed time until they realize they haven't screamed in at least an hour."

The lawyer laughed.

Jed let Camille slide onto the booth seat first, then he sat alongside her, bracing his hand on her thigh. He didn't care if it was politically correct or karmically cool. He needed the emotional support.

She cupped her hand over his, interlocking their fingers.

Her actions warmed him in a way he couldn't begin to describe. She made him feel less alone, even though most of his family was forever gone.

"I'm sorry," Camille said to their guest. "Would you like coffee? A soft drink?"

"No, but thank you. My last doctor visit was less than ideal. It's strictly water for me."

"Water, then?" Jed asked. Anything to avoid learning his sister's wishes. His gut told him she'd left him her girls and he wasn't ready to hear it—might never be ready for such life-altering news.

"If it's not too much trouble." Baxter remained standing as he continued removing forms and pens from his briefcase.

Jed left Camille and the booth to make the short trek to the fridge for three bottled waters—just in case anyone else wanted one.

"Thank you." Baxter accepted the drink, but didn't open it. "Let's get down to business…"

Jed rejoined Camille, interlocking his fingers with hers again. His heart beat uncomfortably fast as the lawyer took a seat beside him. *Please don't gift me your girls, Em. I love them dearly, but as an uncle. Not the way a father should love his daughters.*

"I'll skip the legalese and get straight to the point." *Thump, thump, thump.* Was he having a heart attack? *I'm not ready to be a dad.*
I can't be a dad.

Chapter 10

Baxter cleared his throat. "Interestingly enough, your sister left you the house, with the understanding that she needed you to maintain it for your mother and her daughters. That's the reason we couldn't handle this via phone. Too much paperwork for the deed transfer. She and Chase's life insurance was more than enough to pay off any debts, and the house and acreage has been paid off since your grandparents' time. All that's necessary for you to keep up with—aside from maintenance, of course—are the annual taxes. There is a stipulation in place that should they desire, your mother and the girls are allowed to reside here for the entirety of their lives."

"Of course." *But what about custody? Who's raising the three tenors?*

Baxter assembled a massive stack of papers, feeding them to Jed one at a time to sign. "I'll send copies. Also, I'll have the property deed registered in your name. Since your mom will be assuming primary care for the girls, Emily left her the car and financial bulk of the estate, as well as the girls' college funds."

Wait, what? Jed hadn't been named guardian?

He should have been happy about the fact, but oddly enough he felt somehow ripped off. Had Emily not trusted him to care for her girls? Had she not thought him capable of doing a good job? Considering how a few moments earlier, he'd damn near had a heart attack from the fear of becoming his nieces' legal guardian, he now felt equally disappointed. Which made no sense.

He was losing it.

Correction—maybe he had already lost it?

An hour later, the babies were again screaming, Baxter had left and Jed still sat sullenly at the kitchen table, while Camille prepped bottles.

"What's with the long face?" she asked. "I thought this was what you wanted? For your mom to get the girls?"

"It was—is. But something about hearing it legally stated... I don't know how to describe it. It kind of pissed me off."

"You're acting crazy." She set all three bottles on the table, then proceeded to fetch the babies from their swings. "You can't have it both ways."

"I know. That's what I mean."

"Trust me, once you're back in sunny California, doing whatever it is that you SEALs do, you'll be relieved to have this chapter behind you."

"You're probably right."

"Of course I am." She handed him Sallie, and then Callie.

She took Allie, cradling her, fitting her pinkie into the infant's palm. "Have you ever really looked at them? Their tiny perfection. These fingers…" she said in a soft, singsongy tone. "The itty-bitty nails. It won't be too long till your grandma's going to be a full-time manicurist, once you and your sisters discover nail polish."

"Why do you think she did it?"

"Huh?" Camille looked up from her inspection of his niece.

"Why didn't Emily trust me to care for her girls?"

"Are you listening to yourself?"

"I mean it. I fully expected Baxter to name me guardian and I was steeling myself for it. But when he didn't?" He scowled. "I'm not used to losing. I don't like it—not one bit."

"Gee, that's kind of how I'm feeling about you in this moment—not liking you one bit. How have you so easily forgotten your speech about not feeling capable of being a parent? You and Emily were close. Don't you think she sensed that if, God forbid, something happened to her or Chase—let alone both—that your mom would be most capable of raising the girls?"

"I need air." He fanned himself.

"Good for you, but in case you forgot, you still have two hungry babies in your arms."

He glanced at his hungry charges. "Damn."

"And that right there is why Emily had more faith in your mom…" She tickled Allie's chubby tummy.

"Thought you were on my side?"

"I'm on the side of these three vulnerable infants. We've been over this ad nauseum. Neither of us are parent material. Don't take it personally." When Allie lost the bottle's nipple, she broke into a wail. "Here you go, sweet baby…" Camille had the bottle back in place before Allie finished her last cry. "Nothing to worry about."

"You're good with them—way better than me. Maybe Em should have left the girls with you?"

"Right." Camille laughed. "Because I've had such great experiences with kids in my past."

"What you went through on the job hardly counts."

"Really?" Eyebrows raised, she said, "Well, I was there, and I think it does. All of the infants in my charge are now deceased." With a heavy sigh, she left the booth and kitchen, taking Allie with her.

"Camille, come back!" He gazed at his companions. "You know what, ladies? "I think these last few days have taken their toll on Auntie Camille, too."

Deadpan expressions were their only response.

"All right, well, let's hurry up and finish eating so we can chase after her and see what she needs us to do to get back in her good graces. Agreed?"

They stared as if he were a two-headed alien.

"Did you know that as a SEAL, I've been trained to always have a contingency plan? As such, let's take this show on the road. If Auntie Camille can feed your sister upstairs, we'll do the same. It'll be like a picnic."

Holding the girls extra close while holding their bottles steady, he took the stairs two at a time.

"Cam?"

No answer.

He found her on the daybed in the sun-flooded nursery.

"There you are." He squeezed in alongside her. "Mind if I join you?"

"Yes."

"What's wrong?"

"You. You're all over the map. This is serious, Jed. These girls lost both their parents, and till your mom gets here, we're literally all they have left in the world. There's no telling how long that will take, and until Barbara is home, I need you to step up and get serious. This isn't a game."

"Trust me. More than anyone, I know." A muscle ticked in his hardened jaw. "Did you forget I was the one having to call for an ambulance when Em collapsed? I had to say goodbye to her lifeless form. I get that this isn't a game."

"Then why are you treating it like one?"

"I wasn't aware that I was?"

"Your feelings regarding your nieces seem scattered when you need to be unflappable, for their sakes. One minute, you're caring for them like a seasoned parenting pro, the next, I find you lying on the floor in front of a crib, looking like you're about to cry harder than the girls."

"That was an isolated event. You'd have been near tears, too, had you heard them screaming as long as I did."

"I'm not saying I wouldn't, but Jed, instead of caring for the girls like you already have one foot back on the beach, how about being fully here and committed for as long as it takes for your mom to come home? Instead of wishing yourself to be anywhere but here, how about enjoying this sacred time with three baby girls who desperately need your love and support?"

Jed wanted to be mad at her for the scathing speech, but how could he when every word she'd spoken was true?

Two weeks passed, and with no sign of Jed's mother, Camille would have expected him to grow more antsy about returning to his military life. But if anything, he seemed to have embraced his current role with abandon.

She'd watched the girls while he'd made Emily's cremation arrangements. Her memorial service wouldn't be held till Barbara returned. A weaker man might have cracked under the pressure of being an instant parent while still mourning his sister and brother-in-law's deaths. But he still held strong.

Maybe too strong?

As if his SEAL commander had issued an infant care instruction manual, he'd become as proficient at diaper duty as he was with bath time and making bottles. The one thing missing was heart. As silly as it seemed, she wanted him to stop the mechanics of caring for his nieces in lieu of appreciating them for the miracle they were. For the living memory of Emily and Chase and all the loved ones they'd lost before.

She longed to see him blowing raspberries on tummies and singing off-key lullabies at bedtime. Why didn't he stare in awe at their perfection during feeding times, when she grew more enamored with the trio with each passing day?

"Got everything?" He peeked into the canvas sack she'd been filling for that afternoon's outing to her grandfather's mine. Since the weather had finally fallen into a warmer pattern, most afternoons they'd taken to picnicking either with the horses or up one of the dozen or so trails that both Chase's and Jed's fathers had long-ago cut into the land.

Her grandfather hadn't ended up moving in with them, but to make her life easier, he had started riding his mule, Earl, to dinner at Jed's. Seemed strange, calling Chase and Emily's place his, but legally that was the case.

"I think we have it all," she said. "The only way we'll know for sure is if we get there and discover we need something we don't have." Since her grandfather seemed to get a kick out of spending time with the girls, she thought it might be fun to go on a bigger adventure than their norm, as the mine was a pretty good hike from where they'd leave the SUV.

"True." Jed hefted the bag over his right shoulder. "Ready for me to start loading the girls?"

"Yes, please."

He'd been different since her scolding about his take on the whole custody issue. Cool, but in an ultra-polite way.

She hated it.

The emotional distance between them.

Had her harsh words created it? If so, how could she regret speaking what had needed to be said? His lousy attitude only proved her belief that she wasn't cut out for relationships.

Nothing good lasted.

A lesson her job experience had driven home by the cruelest of means.

All gear loaded, with Jed at the wheel, the five of them set off for the mine. The winding mountain road was beyond treacherous, with drop-offs so steep she closed her eyes during switchback turns.

Allie whimpered, starting a chain reaction of complaints that necessitated George Strait joining their journey.

Higher and higher they traveled, until popping out above the tree line. A few slow and bumpy miles later had Jed turning off onto the even bumpier trail leading to her grandfather's mine.

Jed parked the SUV next to Gramps's old Ford pickup, then killed the engine. The sudden silence startled the girls into a screaming frenzy.

Jed groaned. "It never ends."

"Shush. I swear, you're a bigger baby than all of them combined." She'd meant it as a joke—mostly—but it hadn't landed.

"What's that supposed to mean?"

"Nothing." She opened her door and stepped out onto the gravel. "Sorry I said anything." But she wasn't sorry. Maybe she'd been too direct with him previously, but ever since learning his sister hadn't wanted him to be her daughters' surrogate father, he hadn't been the same. How could he resent a decision he'd claimed to want?

Unless deep down, that hadn't been what he'd wanted at all?

A babbling brook ran alongside a rickety wooden picnic table her grandfather had built when she'd been a little girl.

Earl grazed ten yards up the hill on a patch of clover.

At this altitude, the sky seemed bluer. The sun shone brightly enough for Camille to hold her hand to her forehead, shading her eyes.

"No..." Jed climbed out and slammed his door, rounding the SUV's front to face her. "You brought it up, so explain what you meant."

She said with a sigh, "Drop it before my grandfather comes down. I don't want him to hear us argue."

"It's better than the silent treatment I usually get."

"Oh—that's rich, coming from you."

"Good God almighty..." Her grandfather shouted

from high up on the trail leading to his mine's entrance. "You two make more noise than all three of those little ones put together."

Camille pressed her lips together.

Jed did the same.

Oddly enough, the babies had stopped crying.

"Thought you were comin' to bring me food, not aggravation." Gramps followed the trail down faster than he should have, scattering rocks and pebbles. He wore his antique tin gold pan as a sun hat.

"Ollie, mind watching the girls while I take your granddaughter up to the mine for a private talk?" Jed ran his hand over his hair, which was starting to grow out.

"That won't be necessary," she said. "Gramps, let's just eat."

Her grandfather said, "Why would I want to break bread with two folks who should have been married ten years back, but didn't, yet still fuss like an old married couple?"

Really? Camille crossed her arms, sending her grandfather a dirty look.

"Go on," Gramps said. "I'll keep an eye on the kiddos."

"Thanks." Jed gestured for Camille to go first.

"Who wants to learn how to pan for gold?" After opening the SUV's rear door, her grandfather removed his gold pan to wave it about. His jig elicited excited shrieks from the back seat crew.

"What was that?" Jed nodded toward the girls. "Have you ever heard that noise?"

"It's a new one for me. Apparently, Gramps is a baby whisperer."

"Guess so."

Up and up Camille and Jed climbed on the well-worn trail, until reaching the mine, which her grandfather had shored with railroad ties. He'd worked it for as long as she could remember, riding Earl every day.

"We're here. What do you have to say that couldn't be said in front of Gramps?"

Camille braced her hands on her hips. She wouldn't usually snap at him like this, but honestly, she was sick and tired of his standoffish nature lately. "What's your problem? Before Baxter read Emily's will, I felt like the two of us were in this together, but ever since then, you've been an ass."

"Thanks."

"It's true."

"Look…" He rubbed the back of his neck. "Whatever's going on with me is complicated."

"Try explaining. If there's anyone you can talk to, you should know whatever you need to say is safe with me."

He sat on the hand-hewn log bench just outside the mine.

Cool air swished through the entrance, creating as much of a breeze as a fan. It smelled dank and musty and made her shiver.

"You okay?"

She nodded. Interesting how even in the heat of an argument, Jed held concern for her. She loved that about him. No matter what, he'd always have her back. But that didn't mean he'd have her heart. Things between them had grown way too complicated for that. They hadn't so much as napped in the same room since that night when she'd awakened in his arms. "Let's get this over with. I don't trust the girls with poor Gramps."

Her joke earned a faint smile.

"This is going to sound crazy, but here goes…" He shifted, crossing one leg than the other, as if he was incapable of finding comfort. "You're right, this has everything to do with the will. No way did I ever see myself becoming a dad to triplets, but then the two of us were working together and it shocked me when we made a pretty great team. And there was a part of me that thought about how things used to be between us— how we talked about having kids, and how I wanted a boy to hunt and fish with and you wanted a girl to teach your grandmother's recipes to, and play dress-up, and for a hot minute, I could so clearly see us in those roles. But then I regained my sanity and realized you have your life and I have mine."

She couldn't have said why, but tears stung Camille's eyes. There was so much she wanted—*needed*—to say, but it was so uncharacteristic for Jed to open up like this, she didn't want to stop him.

"I said I wanted Emily to have entrusted her daughters' care to our mom, but then when that's exactly what happened, I was pissed. I wanted to know what was so wrong with me that she wouldn't have wanted them raised by me. Even worse, her message from beyond the grave made me feel like she'd not just gutted me once by practically dying in my arms, but twice by making it public knowledge that she doesn't think I'm capable of taking care of her girls. But I am. These past couple weeks, I've more than proved I can handle anything, from the worst diaper accident to laundry to bath time, and anything else three babies could ever throw my way."

"Oh, Jed…" Dropping to the bench, Camille wrapped her arms around him, needing him to know he was right, but also wrong. He would hate what she had to say, but he needed to hear it. "Yes, when it comes to the girls' physical care, you're incredible—but like the soldier you are. You care for them with an almost robotic precision that's extraordinary, but also a smidge cold."

"Seriously?"

"It's a valid observation." She forged onward. "Do you love them? Your nieces?"

"Of course." On his feet, he strode away from her. "How could you even ask something like that?"

"Sorry. But before we get any deeper, I needed to know."

"You sit there all high and mighty, preaching about me being cold with my own flesh and blood, when you quit a job you fought for because of growing too attached to kids who weren't even alive."

"That was a low blow—even for you." She wiped hot, silent tears with the backs of her hands. She'd demand he take the cruel words back, but how could she when what he said was right?

"I've been abandoned all my life. My dad, my grandmother—"

"I know how that feels, Jed—"

"My brother-in-law and sister. Now, even my nieces are being taken from me. Everyone I love leaves."

Camille had no comeback for that.

"Even you…"

"Point of fact." She raised her chin. "You left me."

"That's bullshit. I asked you to come with me and you wouldn't."

"What life would I have had? Hanging around on a series of navy bases? Commiserating with other wives who were pining for their husbands, too? You know exactly why I didn't go. I owed it to myself to finish college and pursue a career I thought would heal old wounds from my dad's murder."

"You've said yourself that the only thing your detective career did was make you feel more hopeless about what happened to your dad. Did you ever regret choosing your career over me?"

"You got married six weeks after we mutually called it quits! Who does that? Even if I did have regrets back then, what was I supposed to do, track you down when you were with someone else? It makes no sense."

"If you loved me, it makes all the sense in the world."

"Okay—then let's flip that around. If you still loved me, why didn't you come for me?"

At some point during their mutual outbursts, she'd stood, gravitating closer and closer, until Camille now realized they stood toe to toe.

If only they could see eye to eye on the issues that were no closer to being resolved.

Chapter 11

"We should check on the girls," Jed said. As much as he currently couldn't stand the sight of Camille, he was equally too proud to admit that much of what she'd said was right.

"They're fine. As loud as they are, we would hear them if Gramps had run into trouble," she said.

"We're done here."

"Are we?"

He rammed his hands in his jeans pockets. "I have nothing more to say."

"I call bull."

"What do you want from me?"

"Everything!"

He rolled his eyes. How had she forgotten that he'd offered her just that, but she'd flat turned him down?

"What's wrong with you? Do you even have a soul?

I'm the one who left my career because of heartache, yet you reportedly have a great job and life that you love, yet from my point of view, all I see is this cold, lifeless machine."

"Are you kidding me? I cried like my nieces when I learned Emily died."

"Do you want a trophy?"

Jed backed up as if struck.

"I'm sorry," she said, reaching for him.

He grabbed her wrist, drawing her hand to his mouth, where he flipped it over, kissing her palm. "I'm sorry, too. All of this just came out and I don't even know from where. I'm so angry—like deep-down, gut-level furious, and I can't figure out why." He kissed her palm again and again. "Help me, Cam. Help me remember how to feel."

She took his hand, kissing each finger, then his palm.

They stood close enough that Camille could have kissed his lips, but she didn't. She wanted to, but what then? Even if her tin man found his heart, what good would it do her? He wasn't staying in Marigold, and given California's crime, she sure as hell wasn't going there. Just like when they'd called off their engagement, they were at an impossible standoff, with no solution in sight.

"Wish I could help you," she said. "But I'm the last person to ask for advice on remembering how to feel. I've seen husbands lose wives and parents lose children—multiple children to violence so senseless it made me retch. Before leaving my office, I'd routinely pop Dramamine while driving to crime scenes, because I'd tossed my lunch too many times to count."

"Lord…" Jed freed his hand in order to pull her hard against him, kissing the crown of her head, holding her for all he was worth. In this moment, he realized how much she still meant to him. How much she'd always meant. But that fact alone did nothing to patch the hole in his heart. "Has any of this made a difference?"

"I don't think so." Tears welled in her haunting hazel eyes. "The two of us still have drastically different goals and needs for the remainder of our lives. The only thing we do have is this time together until your mom takes over."

"What does that mean?"

"Nothing." She shrugged. "I was just thinking… What if we take this time to play out our every fantasy of what a life together might be like? Since we both know it's a dream that for sheer practicality's sake will never come true, what would it hurt to make believe? Whether for a few days or a few weeks, once it is time for us to again go our separate ways, at least we'll have memories to see us through."

"I like it." He pushed her far enough back to search her face. To tell if this proposal meant as much to her as it did him. "Let me get this straight. We'd be a couple again— in *every* possible way—but only till Mom gets here."

"Right. Deal?" She extended her hand for him to shake. Which he did. But while he still had hold of her, he reeled her close again. And when they shared the very air between them, and his pulse beat loudly enough to hear in his ears, he hovered his lips over hers, asking in a ragged voice, "Sure this is what you want?"

She not only nodded, but closed the gap, pressing her lips to his. She felt so soft, so like his dream of her that he'd carried ever since their last kiss goodbye.

Framing her dear face with his hands, he couldn't get enough of her, parting her lips for a thrilling sweep of their tongues.

She groaned, twining her hands around his neck and into his hair. "I've missed you. *This*."

"Same. But it won't last."

"Can't." The kiss went on and on, as if they'd been starving and then discovered the ultimate all-you-can-eat buffet. "This will be enough."

"Perfect." He meant the kiss, not the plan. She was right about them never being long-term together—there was no arguing that point. But it didn't make it easier to bear. More like the way he dealt with the harsher aspects of SEAL training not because he liked it, but because he didn't have a choice.

"We should get to the babies," she said. "But later…"

"Lord, yes…" He nipped her lower lip, drawing it out, only to kiss her again.

When they next parted for air, she said, "Let's play it cool in front of Gramps. I don't want him to know."

"Wise decision. No sense in anyone thinking we're back together for real."

"Exactly." She smoothed flyaway strands of hair back into her ponytail. Tugged at her pink T-shirt's hem. "Ready to go?"

"No."

She grinned. "Me, neither."

Together again, they touched foreheads, laughing, exchanging exhalations.

"Tonight," he said. "As soon as my nieces drift off to sleep, you and I have a date."

"Mmm…" She kissed him yet again. "I can't wait."

"Let me tell you, once that mountain lion and I locked eyes, I snatched up my rifle and…"

Camille had heard the story of the mountain lion

setting up housekeeping in Gramps's mine more times than she could count. Usually, she enjoyed the embellishments he added with each telling, but at the moment the only topic her mind was capable of focusing on was Jed.

His kiss.

His intent that they become a couple in every possible way. An hour had passed since they'd come down the mountain trail to meet Gramps and the girls for lunch, and it was still all she could think about. "…I kid you not, that mountain lion turned out to be a momma. Not only was she livin' in my mine, but her two cubs, too. Well, I couldn't just…"

Allie fussed in her carrier.

Still listening to Gramps, Jed swept her up and into his arms, blowing a raspberry on her belly along the way. Was this the same man? It was as if their talk, their mutual decision to temporarily live out loud, had breathed new life into him. She liked the change.

So did his niece, who sported a drooling grin.

"Your grandmother—God rest her soul—made up a palette from a bunch of old clothes she was fixing to donate to the church. It was a lucky thing that the momma was in a played-out shaft, otherwise I might not have been so generous in sharing my claim."

"You ever see her mate?" Jed asked.

"Nah." Gramps scratched his wiry white beard. "But I will never forget the day she brought me a squirrel by way of thanks."

"No way…" Had Jed not heard the story as many times as she had? Or was he being polite? Regardless, Camille enjoyed seeing her two favorite men together. "How long did she stay?"

"Just till winter's end. After that, I never saw any of them again—well, correction. There was that time when she saved me from what I'm pretty doggoned sure was a Bigfoot." He winked at Camille. "But that story might be too scary for the wee ones, so I'll save it for another day."

Camille wouldn't have minded more stories.

With their picnic of deviled eggs, fried chicken and potato salad spread out on the pretty calico tablecloth she'd found among Emily's linens, Camille would be hard-pressed to recall a day from recent memory that had been more sublime. From the balmy weather to the company, happiness wasn't just within reach, but hers for the taking—for a little while. It would be fleeting, but enough to get her through the dark times sure to come once Jed was gone.

While all three took a baby to feed from the bottles Camille had also packed, Jed and Gramps shared war stories—Jed from Iraq and her grandfather from the tail end of WWII.

Even the girls seemed lulled by warm sun and the carefree mood of the day. They'd grown in the short time she'd been with them. Emily had penciled in a well-child visit on the kitchen calendar for next week. The babies would be a smidge over three months.

Developmentally, she had so much to look forward to. Even after Jed's mom returned, Camille planned to stay and help. Maybe she could even sweet-talk her mother into making a visit.

With Sallie in her arms, Camille took a handful of carrot sticks from the relish tray, then left the guys swapping stories. She'd rather visit with Earl.

"Hey, buddy." She approached him nice and slowly. "Hungry?"

Hee-haw, hee-haw! He'd sniffed the carrots, nudging her hand before she'd even offered them.

Sallie held out her tiny hand, wide-eyed at being this close to the creature.

"Want to pet him?"

The baby bucked in Camille's arms, drooling, opening and closing her mouth like a little fish.

"You're wanting to taste him, aren't you?" she said with a laugh. "Earl's a patient mule, but I'm not sure how he'd feel about being used for a teething ring."

She helped Sallie pet Earl, who was so busy chewing carrot sticks that he didn't seem to mind inquisitive baby fingers grabbing hold of his ear.

"Girl," her grandfather said, "I've eaten so much that I think Earl and me should go home for a nap."

"Want a ride?" Jed asked. "I could come back for Earl with Chase's horse trailer."

"Nope. But I appreciate the offer. What should I do with this little lady?" He tugged the brim of Allie's pink sun hat.

"I'll take her." Jed placed Callie in her carrier, then reached for her sister.

"Thank you, young man." Gramps yawned. "She's heavier than she looks. My arm was getting sore."

Jed laughed. "Try holding all three at once."

"Can't even imagine." Gramps took his gold pan from the table, put it on his head, sauntered to Earl, hopped on him bareback, then waved. "We'll see y'all for supper tomorrow."

Camille moved Sallie's arm in a wave.

"That was fun." Jed fastened the plastic lid on the

deviled egg platter. "He's a great guy. Makes me see where you got your spunk. I'm gonna have to hear that Bigfoot story."

"Promise, you don't want to hear."

Snagging her around her waist, he pulled her in for a long, leisurely kiss. "Mmm... Didn't think anything could top your deviled eggs, but that was before I'd had another taste of you."

"Where is Jed and what did you do with him?"

"Ate him along with the last of the chicken." His deadpan delivery, followed by a sexy wink was classic Jed. The one she'd fallen in love with all those years ago and could all too easily fall for again.

Charming Jed was dangerous for her heart...

"Divide and conquer?" Jed asked once they got home. All he could think about was their new arrangement. How brilliant it was. All the benefits of the future he'd always imagined with Camille, with none of the catastrophic long-term results—namely, her leaving him. This way, with them both on the same page about the end date, that effectively ended his worries, allowing him to see just far enough into the future to know the break from her was coming, but since he knew ahead of time, it would be no big deal, right? "I'll check the livestock and you handle baby stuff."

"Deal." Still in the SUV's front seat, she thrust out her hand for him to shake, which he did. But that wasn't enough of her—not nearly enough. Proven by his damn near instant erection. "But help me get the girls to the kitchen first."

"Sure." Patience had never been his strong suit, but in this case, it wasn't like he had a choice.

Jed helped arrange his nieces for Camille's feeding assembly line, then trekked to the barn.

Lucy and Ethel grazed at the far end of the pasture on tender new grasses, but in case they got hungry later, he put out hay and freshened their water. It would be warm enough that they wouldn't need to stay inside, but he left their pen open in case they wanted shelter.

The chickens seemed crankier than usual, with lots of warbling and pecking. They'd made a mess of the coop floor, meaning in good conscience, he had to give it a sweep.

The goats seemed happy to see him, so they got extra grain and the table scraps Camille had stashed in the fridge from last night's dinner. She was always thoughtful like that—thinking of everyone, including animals, before herself.

She was great with her grandfather and his nieces. In a way, he wondered if her seeing so many lousy parents over the course of her law enforcement career had helped her internalize what it took to be a good parent.

He was thankful she'd called him out on what uncle skills were most lacking—the warmth. He had been afraid to fully invest his emotions in the girls, the same way he was with Camille. But no more.

All four ladies in his life deserved his best, and Jed was determined to give it.

Inside, he found Camille seated in the kitchen booth with the babies lining the table in their carriers. She held two bottles and used the old dishrag trick to prop the third.

"That was fast," she said. "How's the barn crew?"

"Good—except for the chickens. I don't think they like me."

"Oh?" She raised her brows. "How can you tell?"

"It's a gut feeling."

She laughed. "You're crazy."

"Probably."

They'd always bantered, but tonight the energy was different. Supercharged as if they both anticipated what was to come.

"I vote we skip bath time," he said.

"We can't do that. They're all dusty from being outside for so long."

He pretended to inspect Allie. "She looks clean to me."

"It's not even five. If we put them to bed now, we'll be up all night."

"Thought that was the plan?" He winked.

She sighed. "About that…"

"Nope. Don't you dare renege on our deal."

"I'm not. It's just that…" She averted her gaze.

"What?"

"I want to—you know. But it's been an awfully long time and I'm not even sure—"

"Stop right there. It's not as if I've been scoring major action in Syria."

"I don't like the thought of you purposely going to dangerous places."

Shrugging, he said, "That's kind of my job."

"How would your mother survive if something happened to you, too?" She swiped at silent tears. "Look at me, I'm an instant mess just thinking about it."

"Babe…" Seated beside her on the booth seat, he slipped his arm around her shoulders, holding her close. "I'm good at what I do. That's not to say accidents don't happen, but that's the last thing you need to worry about."

"Easy for you to say. You'd be gone, but I'd be here picking up the pieces of the emotional train wreck that used to be your mom."

"Wait a minute…" Forehead furrowed, he asked, "How did the topic switch from grown-up fun time to me dying and you assuming full-time care of my mom? And presumably the babies?"

"Somebody has to care for them."

Callie's bottle slipped. Her red-faced screaming fury told the world she wasn't happy about it.

"Could we please focus on the here and now rather than my tragic future?"

Camille nodded.

It took fifteen minutes of beyond awkward silence for the tenors to finish their bottles.

From there, it was another thirty from the start of bath time till everyone was dried, diapered and cuddled.

Back in the den, Jed sat with Camille alongside the girls' activity mat. Before Chase died, Emily had been an online shopping fanatic, scoring big time with toys and baby gear. He showed a black-and-white fabric pattern book to Allie, but she seemed more intrigued by her sister's toes.

"Want me to make a fire?" Jed asked.

"No, thank you. It was such a pretty day, I don't feel like it's cold enough."

"How about some popcorn? We didn't have dinner."

"You're right. We forgot."

"Is that a yes to popcorn?" He jingled a turquoise dolphin that had a bell on its nose.

Sallie yawned.

"Thanks, but I'd rather have something more substantial. How do you feel about omelets?"

"Good. Should we pop the girls in their swings and I'll help cook?"

"Sure. Thanks."

Midway through the process, he asked, "Do you ever feel like we're living in that old movie *Groundhog Day*, where the same thing just happens over and over?"

"I think that's called parenthood."

"But isn't something supposed to happen?"

"Just my opinion, but I think the point of not only having kids, but life, is to live in the moment and enjoy the little things." She sprinkled cheddar cheese over the diced ham and green onion mixture she'd already layered over the beaten eggs. "Like the smell of ooey-gooey melting cheese. Or the way all three girls hold their left arm out on every swing forward."

"How'd you get so wise?" Behind her, he nuzzled the back of her neck.

"Years of college I'm still paying for."

"Ahh… You smell incredible."

"I smell like sweat and dirt and baby spit."

"And you…" He reached around her to take the pan off the stove, then turned her to face him. The deep V of her T-shirt invited him to kiss her sweat-sheened chest, moving up to graze his lips across her arched throat.

"Should we be doing this in front of the babies?"

"No clue…" He raised his attention to her lips. Her crazy full and sexy-sweet lips that he'd craved since earlier today.

He glanced over her shoulder to find all three kid-dos sleeping. Gesturing that way, he said, "Look…"

"Think it's a sign?"

"For us to finally have the reunion that's been years in the making? Hell, yes."

They carried the girls to the nursery, placing them all in the same crib, covering them with their mother's blanket.

Jed checked the monitor on his way out of the room, then pocketed the handset.

"We're free," Camille said, with a long, slow exhale.

"What do you want to do?" Was his tone too suggestive? He wanted her—all over—with a physical ache. But he wasn't getting the same desperation vibe from her. What did that mean? Was she regretting her idea of their temporary hook-up?

"Let's eat," she said.

Her expression unreadable, she held out her hand to him.

He took it, appreciating the connection—however brief.

They ate at the booth.

Camille had turned on folksy rock he didn't recognize. No offense, but anything would have been preferable to the George Strait tune his nieces favored.

"Know what I regret?" he said, between forkfuls of her delicious meal.

"No clue." She sipped the sun tea she'd had brewing on the front porch all afternoon.

"Not taking you to prom."

"That would've been awfully tough, considering my high school was in Miami and yours was here."

"I know, but I should've saved up my allowance to fly you in. I figured we'd finally get to dance at our wedding, but that didn't pan out, either."

"Let's do it now." She held out her hand to him.

"For real?"

"Why not?"

Having no argument, he took her hand, easing her out of the booth and onto the highly polished pine plank kitchen floor. They'd both ditched their boots and only wore thick white socks. Not the most elegant of looks, but it worked for him.

He settled his palms low on her slender hips, and he loved the feel of her hands exploring his back. The music had taken on a dreamy quality that perfectly suited his mood.

Tired, but hopeful.

Expecting nothing, but *everything*.

Chapter 12

Camille tried playing it cool, but how could she when she'd literally waited a lifetime to be once again held like this in Jed's strong arms?

During their brief engagement, they'd been too young to appreciate the magic of what they'd shared. Now, after being back with him for just a couple weeks, she wondered if not going with him after his basic training had been her life's biggest mistake. Not that she could correct that—just that she had a sneaking suspicion that for a long time to come, no matter what paths their separate lives led, she'd always look back on this brief, tragic yet exhilarating time as one of the most special in her life.

Did that make her a bad person? Without two of her dearest friends dying, she never would have landed in this position.

But here she was, being led in her stocking feet around Emily's serene country kitchen, and she couldn't have been more content.

The song ended with Jed landing the sweetest, softest kiss on her lips. "Thank you. That was nice."

"Yes, it was." She looked down, unsure what to do with her hands. Her runaway pulse had galloped all the way to Aspen and her palms were damp with sweat. "Jed?"

"Yeah?"

"Would you be mad at me if instead of going straight to bed, we hung out a little? Maybe watched a movie and had that popcorn you earlier offered?"

"Mad at you?" He laughed, tucking flyaway strands of hair behind her ears. "The only thing that would make me mad is if you complain about me putting too much butter on my signature popcorn."

"Too much butter?" She raised her brows. "Trust me, those are words you'll never hear from me."

The night only got better from there.

They laughed through the latest Will Ferrell comedy and grew teary during a surprisingly heartfelt sci-fi.

What Camille struggled with was the rising tension that had nothing to do with movies and everything to do with expectations for what came after. She knew Jed was expecting to go all the way, but she wasn't sure she was ready. Oh, she was 1000 percent sure she wanted him, but she also wanted their reunion to be special— not just a quick romp in the proverbial hay.

Was she being overly sentimental?

Was she asking for too much?

Times like these she'd once turned to friends like Emily for advice, but with her gone and Camille's Miami friends drifting off, the deeper into depression she'd sunk until there was no one left to turn to—certainly not her mom, who was old-fashioned enough to believe women shouldn't have sex before marriage. If Camille had abided by that rule, she'd be the oldest living virgin.

From the monitor came the sound of one of the babies crying.

"Want me to go?" Camille asked, pressing Pause on the movie.

"Let me." He left the monitor on the coffee table.

Next, came the thumps of him taking the stairs two at a time.

From the monitor, she heard him as clearly as if she were in the nursery with him.

"Hey, Callie cupcake," he said in an adorable croon. Camille's mind's eye saw him take the baby from the crib, cradling her close. "What's the problem?" There was a pause, then, "Diaper's dry. It's not time for your late-night snack. Needing a cuddle?"

The whimpers quieted, and then came the most precious thing she'd ever heard…

"Hush, little baby, don't say a word, Uncle Jed's gonna buy you a big green bird. I don't know the words to this song, but hopefully you won't know if I'm wrong. I love you and I hope you love me, you're pretty lucky to be part of a group of three…"

Her heart melted.

Why had Jed hidden this tender side? Why didn't he want her to know that he cared for the girls as much as she did?

He returned five minutes later.

She'd tried reading a magazine, but had been on the same page for most of the time he'd been gone.

"Everything okay?" she asked.

"Fine. The wind kicked up. She was probably spooked by a branch against the window. I'll get the ladder out tomorrow and trim the branches back."

"Good."

There was so much she wanted to talk to him about. Whether he felt like it would be hard walking away from the babies, with whom they'd grown so close. She tried telling herself leaving them in Barbara's more-than-capable care would be no big deal, but what if she was wrong?

"Where were we?" he asked, pressing Play on their sci-fi movie.

"I think the Undersea Kingdom warriors were on the verge of rescuing their queen."

"Right." He lost himself in the movie, but it no longer held her interest. The only thing she wanted was to get lost in him. To forget her job and the pain of losing him and never finding another man who'd in any way remotely measured up to him.

Leaving her side of the sofa, she went to him, straddling him, pressing her superheated core against his fly. She dragged off his shirt, kissing his pecs and collarbone and throat.

He grabbed her upper arms, pushing her lightly back. "You sure?"

Camille nodded.

With the movie still playing, casting the dark room in chaotic lights and shadows, he removed her T-shirt and bra, then dipped low to take one of her nipples into his mouth, sucking hard enough that she felt the drawing need between her legs.

He unbuttoned her jeans, easing down the zipper,

then helping her wriggle them past her hips and thighs, taking her panties along for the ride.

While kissing her, he strummed his fingers along her core, stroking her, entering her, making her wild with need. She rode his fingers and then he was ripping at his fly, freeing himself enough so that she could slide atop him. It had been so long that at first his size hurt, but then she stretched and molded to him, hungering for even more.

She no longer recognized the needy mews emerging from her throat.

When he thrust up, she bore down.

The pleasure of it drove her wild.

He was kissing her again, plunging his hand into the hair at the nape of her neck that had long since escaped its ponytail holder.

Outside, wind howled, but inside, all that mattered was riding him faster and harder until her every tension released in a white-hot burst of pure, heady sensation.

Breathing heavily, she collapsed against him and he held her, whispering the sweetest words about how much he'd missed her and how in her arms he felt as if he'd finally found home.

With her still clinging to him, he awkwardly struggled to his feet.

Shrieking, she asked, "What are you doing?"

"Taking us to the shower, where we're having an epic do-over."

She kissed him again. "Carry on, cowboy."

The day had arrived for the girls' well-child check, and Camille couldn't have been more nervous than if she were back in college taking an exam.

The girls chilled in their stroller, but she and Jed shared a love seat in the Aspen pediatrician's waiting area. Because Emily's pregnancy and delivery had been high risk, the doctor had been at the delivery, along with her ob-gyn.

The office catered to not only locals, but the children of elite tourists visiting the legendary ski destination. A massive saltwater fish tank took up an entire wall. The opposite wall held an assortment of old-school arcade games and pinball machines. On the far end of the vaulted-ceilinged room towered a massive window through which sunlight streamed.

"Relax." Jed placed his hand on Camille's jiggling right leg. "You act like you're getting an exam."

"I know. What if the doctor finds something wrong? What if we haven't been feeding them enough or—"

A door opened on the only side of the room not tricked out for kid pleasure.

A nurse dressed in tie-dyed pink scrubs stepped through and consulted her chart. "Sallie, Callie and Allie."

"Relax," Jed said again. "They're going to be fine and so are you." They got up to follow the nurse into the exam room.

"Yikes." The nurse eyed the two diaper bags Camille carried along with her purse. "Do you need help?"

"We're good." Jed steered the stroller down a sky-blue corridor lined with Aspen's hot air balloon festival prints.

"At this point," Camille said, "we're so good at hauling baby gear we could start our own moving business."

The nurse laughed, pausing before a long counter. "Before seeing the doctor, let's get weights and vitals."

One at a time, she placed the babies on a digital infant scale, then measured their length—or at least attempted to. Seemed like the girls grew more active with each passing day.

"Are they a normal size for their age?"

"In the seventieth percentile for triplets, so yes—you and their daddy are doing a great job."

"Oh—we're not their parents."

"I'm their uncle. Their parents..."

"I'm so sorry," the nurse said. "I recall hearing the doctor mentioning your case. That must be why you're in later than he usually likes. We see most newborns sooner, but no worries." She ushered them into a room with black-and-white zebra print on the walls, polka-dotted curtains and white vinyl-covered chairs.

"Whoa..." Camille fought the urge to blink.

"I know." The nurse winced. "Since we see only infants in this room, the doctor likes it mentally stimulating so our babies are alert."

"Nailed it," Jed mumbled. He parked the stroller next to the exam table.

"I'm not sure if you're aware," the nurse said, "but the girls will be getting quite a few vaccinations today. I always tell our parents it hurts them more than their kids, but I did want to give you a heads-up."

"Thanks." Camille fussed with the girls' matching, color-coded unicorn shirts.

"You're welcome." The nurse left the room, pausing on the threshold to say, "The doctor should be in soon."

Camille waited a few seconds to be sure they were alone, then freaked. "They're jabbing needles into our girls' tiny little arms and legs and fannies?"

"I'm not sure of the logistics." Sallie fussed, so Jed

plucked her from the stroller. "But you heard the nurse. It won't hurt them too bad and it's kind of a big deal."

"Still…" She nibbled her lower lip in conjunction with jiggling her leg.

"Stop." With his hand on her leg, he said, "What was going through your head when the nurse assumed we're married and the girls are ours?"

"I was mostly caught off guard. Do you think she could tell we're pretending to have a relationship?"

Grinning, he shook his head. "I doubt she cares one way or the other. This is Aspen. I'm sure she's seen about every configuration of parents it's possible to see."

"True…"

He slid his fingers between hers. "Would it make you feel better if I promised ice cream when we're done?"

"What flavor?"

"Chocolate. Is that still your favorite?"

She nodded, touched he remembered.

"It's a date," he said.

She held his hand tighter, wishing they were on a date instead of at a milestone doctor's appointment that Chase and Emily rightfully should have been here for. It wasn't fair. Especially when they'd had so much to look forward to seeing with their baby girls. First smiles and words and steps. So many firsts, yet for Emily and Chase, they'd tragically witnessed their lasts.

A double knock sounded on the door, then a young, handsome doctor with a movie star's perfect smile strolled through. "I remember you," he said to the girls. Gotta love Aspen. Even the pediatricians were larger than life. "You little vixens gave me quite a scare." He tickled tummies while he talked.

The girls gave him their best gummy, drooling grins.

"I recommend C-sections for most of my multiples." He glanced up to Camille and Jed. "But your sister was determined to have them naturally. It was a helluva long night, but she did it. I was so sorry to hear of her and her husband's passing."

"Thanks," Jed said. "It came as a shock to us all."

"They were good people. Real salt of the earth." He looked to his tiny patients, then sat on a rolling stool that he wheeled the short distance to a desktop computer. After pulling up the triplets' charts, he said, "They're looking great. I worried about failure to thrive—that happens sometimes when babies grieve—but whatever you two are doing, keep it up."

Was it wrong that Camille's heart doubled in size with pride?

Jed still held her hand and she was glad.

"Developmentally," the doctor said, "are you starting to see more smiles? More fun noises like cute coos instead of mostly cries?"

She and Jed nodded at the same time.

"Good." He typed a note into the online chart. Wheeling alongside the babies, he clapped just outside of their view.

All three girls turned to check on the sudden noise.

"Perfect," the doctor said. "Their hearing seems good and I like that they have the cognitive skills to follow the sound." He took a hot pink rubber duck from the counter, then rolled his stool to the front of the stroller. He made a few squeaks, moving it from side to side while watching the girls' reaction. "Fantastic. See how they're tracking? They're actually ahead of schedule for this skill." Back at the computer, he made more notes.

"How about when they're on their activity mat for play-time—are you noticing them lifting their heads? Maybe kicking more when they're on their backs?"

"For sure." Jed chuckled. "I'm dreading the day when they're mobile. My sister's house is going to be a night-mare to babyproof."

"Start now," the doctor advised. "They grow fast and will be crawling and then walking before you know it."

The thought saddened Camille. Not because she wasn't happy for the girls, but the thought of not being with them for the milestones shattered her heart.

"Since everything looks great on my end, I'll send in the nurse for their vaccinations. We'll do DTaP, which wards off diphtheria, tetanus and pertussis. From there, Hib for haemophilus influenzae type b, a little IPV which is the inactivated poliovirus. PCV for pneumo-coccal. And last, RV for rotavirus, which is an oral vaccine. Since their momma brought them for their one-month visit, they've already had HepB. Any questions?"

"So many," Camille said with a faint smile. "I'm more than a little overwhelmed. I should have made a list while we were still home. Now, I'm so flustered by the thought of the girls getting shots that I can't re-member a thing."

"That's fairly common," the doctor said, with another of his supersized smiles. "Tell you what, if you get home and think of what you wanted to ask, give us a call."

"I will. Thanks."

"Are you two permanent guardians?"

Jed froze. His expression hardened. "My sister left the girls to our mother. As soon as she returns from her latest mission, she'll be assuming the girls' pri-mary care."

"Good. I'm glad there's a plan in place." He shook their hands, reiterated how it had been nice to meet them and that the nurse would be in to administer the vaccines, and then he was gone.

"Why did Emily do this?" Jed asked when they were alone. "Did she find something in me lacking?"

"Did you ever think that, first off, she never planned on dying only weeks after the girls were born? And second, all you've ever wanted was to be in the navy. It seems fairly logical to me that she wouldn't want to saddle you with this kind of responsibility."

"I guess. Still…" He sighed. "It stings."

"I'm sure." She'd be lying if she said she hadn't harbored fantasies about the two of them raising the triplets together these past weeks. She'd be an aunt, but the girls would consider her their real mom. It wasn't that Camille ever wanted to replace Emily in their hearts, but daughters needed their mother. Part of her felt ready to assume that role. Her time with Jed and her grandfather and the babies had been the perfect medicine to take her mind off what she'd been through in Miami.

Even a month ago, she'd have never believed the peace now residing in her soul, but with Jed and their new little family, life was looking better than it ever had.

At least until all three girls shrieked in horror from receiving shot after shot.

Jed held them during the procedures.

Camille comforted and cooed once it was over.

In the SUV, all three tenors continued wailing until Camille connected her phone to the stereo, blasting George Strait.

"Thank God for George," Jed said, while navigating the crowded medical plaza parking lot.

The girls were already quieting.

"Amen."

"Where should we go for ice cream?"

She covered a yawn. "Thanks for the offer, but I'm good. At this point, I'd rather have a nap."

And time. More than anything, she needed more time with the girls. And most especially, with Jed.

Chapter 13

Another week passed, and though Jed would never admit it, he was in no hurry for his mom to get back. She'd borrowed a SAT phone and explained that flash floods had washed out a few vital bridges. They were too far out of range for helicopters and there were no landing strips for bush planes. He told her to take her time. He and Camille had settled into a routine and were managing just fine.

Well... Better than fine.

Which was why he was up at the crack of dawn checking on Lucy and Ethel and the goats and demon chickens, because he had a special surprise planned for his girls. Make no mistake, at some point in the past month, Camille and his nieces had become an integral part of his life.

One day soon his mom would ride in to the rescue,

taking over in her oh-so-capable way. But until then, he was following Camille's advice and living every moment to the fullest. He was enjoying the girls' every burp and coo, and the way they'd started grinning when he blew raspberries on their chubby bellies. They were growing right before his eyes, as were his feelings for Camille.

He knew that when it was time to head back to base the pain stemming from leaving them would be inevitable, but at least he'd have his memories.

That would be enough, right?

The sudden pain in his stomach hit like a punch. He ignored it. He'd deal with the downside of this arrangement when the time came. Until then, today was about fun.

Entering through the back door, he found Camille at the stove, flipping eggs. A platter of bacon sat on the table, along with juice. All three babies wiggled in their carriers and Camille's grandfather occupied the booth.

"Hey, Ollie." Jed removed his cowboy hat, setting it on the counter along with the basket of eggs he'd gathered. "I didn't know you were here. Where's Earl?"

"Parked him out front," the older man said. "Noticed your yard could use a trim. That's the one downside of this warmer weather—damn lawns."

Jed laughed.

"How's the barn crew?" Camille asked. "And do you gentlemen want one egg or two?"

"I'll take three, please." Jed sat across from Ollie. "Those damn chickens will be the death of me. Two escaped and I had to chase them back into the pen."

"If he's having three eggs," Ollie said, "I'll need

four. Mining takes a lot more effort than gathering a few eggs."

"Hey—those hens are dangerous."

"Whatever."

Camille added more eggs and butter to the frying pan after removing the three that were already done. She put them on a plate that she delivered along with a fork and napkin to Jed. "Gramps, yours are cooking."

"But he gets served before me?" Ollie scowled. "What happened to age before beauty?"

"Thanks, Ollie." Jed snagged a few pieces of bacon. "Good to know you find me attractive."

The old man huffed.

"Ready for your surprise?" he asked Camille.

"I was ready about an hour ago."

"Sorry—those damned chickens are always causing more trouble than they're worth."

"When I was your age," Ollie said, "I could tackle morning chores in under fifteen minutes before the sun even came up. I'd be to the mine before six—all year round. Think a little snow stopped me or Bonkers?" He snorted. "You'd be wrong."

"Gramps, you are such a fibber." Camille set his plate, napkin and fork in front of him. "Grandma told me that when it snowed, you pretended to go to the mine, but you and Bonkers hung out in the nice and toasty tack room, watching your VCR collection of old Westerns and war movies. She said you even had a stash of junk food and bourbon out there."

"I would never call my beautiful wife—God bless her soul—a liar, but not a lick of that is true." He dug into his eggs but aimed a wink in Jed's direction.

"While I always appreciate having history rewritten," she said, "Jed, what's my surprise?"

"Voilà!" He took folded sheets of paper from his Wranglers' back pocket and handed them to her. "We're taking a mini-road trip."

She unfolded the paper to find directions to the Denver Zoo. Excitement swelled in her chest. "You remembered. I haven't been to a zoo since—"

"We used to go together?"

She clapped, then kissed his cheek. "Thank you. Gramps? You want to tag along with me, Jed and the girls?"

Ollie made a face. "Appreciate the invite, but me and Earl have a full schedule." He ate faster. "I've got a good feeling about the motherlode…"

"Aww… Look at the girls looking at the giraffe. Have you ever seen a more adorable sight?" She took a half-dozen more pics on her iPhone. At the rate she was going, she'd run out of memory before they made it even halfway around the zoo.

The temperature was spring perfection in the high seventies, and everywhere she looked leaves were budding and tulips showed off in brilliant swatches of red, yellow and orange.

"Want ice cream?" Jed asked.

"We just had hot dogs."

"And?"

She laughed. "Absolutely. I would love ice cream. Chocolate, please."

"Excellent answer." He steered the stroller toward the Kamalá Café. "I've been dying to see the girls' reaction to trying flavors besides formula."

"Is that safe?" She hustled behind him.

"I'm not talking about giving them their own cones—just licks."

"In that case, sounds fun." The day had been sublime. She'd dressed the girls in matching sun suits—color-coded so they knew who was who. And judging by the crowd reaction to identical triplets, you'd have thought they were movie stars. There had been lots of pointing and staring and even requests for selfies.

Jed gobbled up the attention.

The eatery's air-conditioning felt wonderful, as the day had grown warmer than she'd thought. She lifted her long hair, fanning her neck. Why hadn't she packed a scrunchie?

"Keep exposing your neck like that," Jed whispered, "and we're going to have trouble."

"Oh?" The past few nights she'd grown intimately acquainted with his brand of trouble and she liked it. She teased, "And what do you plan on doing with your nieces during this trouble?"

"Let me think on it. I haven't gotten that far into my plan." He kissed the nape of her neck, making her shiver. She hadn't dreamed it was possible to want a man to this degree—at least not until reuniting with Jed. Which was great, but what did that say about the rest of her life?

Ignoring the question for which she had no answer, she moved with Jed up a few feet in the line.

"Are those triplets?" a pigtailed girl asked. Camille guessed she was around six or seven.

"They sure are." Did Jed realize his chest puffed out each time someone asked? "They're awesome, huh?"

"Super cool!" the girl said with a big nod. "Can I take a selfie with them?"

"I don't mind," he said, "but you should probably ask their mom." Leaning in, he whispered to Camille, *"Go with it."*

"Sure," she replied, not certain why Jed wanted her to play along. "Take all the selfies you want."

"Cool! Thanks!" The girl, wearing a Cinderella T-shirt and plastic crown, whipped her phone from her pink skirt's pocket, then leaned in for a few different poses. "I have to get the best one for my Snapchat!"

Once she'd gone, Jed noted, "When we were that age, we didn't even have phones, let alone social media."

"I know, right? I'm suddenly feeling old."

"For the record," he was back to whispering in her ear, "you're the sexiest old lady I've ever seen."

"Thank you." Considering the G-rated crowd, she kissed his cheek. "I think?"

When their turn finally arrived, they carried the cones to a shaded picnic table.

"This is gonna be great." Jed held his cone to Allie, touching it to her tongue. She froze for a moment, as if unsure what to think, then her adorable face broke into a grin. "I'll take that as a sign she likes it?"

"Absolutely." Camille held her cone to Sallie and earned the same positive reaction.

Jed gave Callie a turn, but she didn't seem at all sure that she was a fan. Her face puckered as if she'd eaten a lemon.

"Every party has a pooper." Jed wiped the melting mini-blob of ice cream mixed with drool from her chin. He repeated the action with the other two girls, then tickled all their tummies.

Camille couldn't get enough of this version of Jed, the ultimate family man. She couldn't remember the last time she'd felt more at ease. At peace with her world. Not only had he and the girls done that for her, but this place had. She'd always loved Colorado and especially the Denver Zoo. It had changed so much over the years as to hardly be recognizable from the one they'd visited as kids, but the spirit was the same. It was the way the world was supposed to be. Fun and safe and a happy place for couples and families and friends.

The fact that Jed brought her here meant so much. It meant he'd remembered her fears and knew this was one place where they could enjoy their day without threat of violence.

Her old life seemed a million miles away.

Exactly where she wanted it.

Even when Jed returned to the navy, as much as she'd miss him, it was good to know she and Barbara and maybe even Ollie could bring the babies here for safe outings off the mountain.

They spent another four hours showing the tenors elephants and tigers and lions and monkeys. They made it through a feeding and diaper changes like seasoned pros, and honestly, Camille did feel like the girls' mom.

They were in the SUV with Jed at the wheel and the girls asleep in their backseat carriers when Camille asked, "When we were at the restaurant, why did you have me tell that girl the babies were mine? Ours?"

"Easy." He took her hand, gliding his fingers between hers. "It was my selfish way of maintaining the illusion that we're a real family." He brought her hand to his mouth, kissing the back, then turning it over to kiss her palm. "This plan of yours—for us to be a couple till Mom gets here—was the most genius idea ever."

"Glad you approve." She leaned her head against the

headrest, turning her face for the awe-inspiring view. Had there ever been a more handsome man? His strong profile made her pulse quicken. And the thought of what they'd probably end up doing after feeding and bath time made her heart pound even faster.

She hoped Barbara showed up soon, because Camille was starting to have a very real fear that if she kept up this temporary relationship much longer, she'd have a tough time letting go.

"I want to top off the tank." Before veering onto the highway, Jed pulled up to a convenience store gas pump. "Mind running in to grab me a coffee and a Slim Jim—one of those extra spicy ones?"

"With coffee?" She made a face. "Want me to also buy a roll of Tums?"

"No, thanks." He patted his T-shirt's chest pocket. "Got 'em right here."

"You're crazier than Gramps."

"A lot better looking, too."

Laughing, she fished her purse out from under the front seat, checked to make sure the babies were still sleeping, then jogged into the store.

She found Jed's spicy meat, then aimed for the coffee stand, also fixing one for herself. Jed preferred black, but she liked cream and lots of sugar.

Passing the candy aisle, she grabbed a handful of green apple Laffy Taffy and a Snickers, then stood in line at the checkout behind an elderly couple and two teens.

Air Supply blared over the store intercom, but she'd have sworn she heard one of the teens tell the clerk to hand over the cash register's money.

No way.

Her imagination was getting the better of her.

"Hand it over, you little pussy!" One of the skinhead teens whipped a 9mm from his hoodie pocket, waving it at the teen clerk.

Though bile rose in Camille's throat, the cop in her switched to autopilot.

The elderly couple backed far enough away to allow Camille to get closer to the perps.

"Give me the money," the taller of the two said, "or I'll shoot you for the fun of it."

"I already told you—" the clerk held up his trembling hands "—there's hardly anything in the register. All the big bills are in the safe and I can't open it."

"Liar." The thug again waved the gun.

"Give us whatever you got." The gunman's pimple-faced friend pulled out a buck knife.

Camille's every instinct screamed for her to run, but her training said the opposite.

Standing next to a counter, she soundlessly dropped the candy and Slim Jim to remove the lids from the two coffees.

"Stop staring and hand over the friggin' money!"

"Excuse me…" Summoning her every ounce of nerve, Camille cleared her throat.

Both teens turned to her.

The one with the gun asked, "What the hell do you want, bitch?"

Without thinking, Camille flung the hot coffees into the teens' eyes.

The kid with the gun popped off a couple rounds at the ceiling before dropping to the floor, writhing in pain.

His buddy soon followed. "My eyes! You whore! I'm blind!"

"Got any duct tape or twine?" Camille asked the clerk. "Anything I can use to tie these guys' hands till help arrives?"

The clerk, evidently in shock, stared at her as if she'd sprouted three heads.

"Cam?" The store's entry burst open and Jed ran inside. "You okay?"

"Fine. Help me find something to bind these idiots' hands."

"D-duct tape," the clerk finally said. "A-aisle five. On the bottom next to the motor oil."

"Thanks," Jed took off in that direction.

"Who's with the babies?" Camille called after him.

"The lady who was using the pump behind me. She's an ER nurse on her way to her shift. She already called 9-1-1."

By the time Jed tied both teens' hands behind their backs, leaving them prone on the floor, police arrived to take over.

They asked Camille far too many questions for her liking, when all she wanted to do was curl into a fetal position with Jed holding her tight. Why had this happened? Just when she'd started to feel safe. Just when she'd seen a glimpse of hope for a brighter future, she now knew it had all been an illusion.

She was no safer here than she had been in Miami. And neither were Emily and Chase's babies or Jed.

More than anything, she'd wanted to believe there was good in the world.

Boy, had she been wrong.

An hour later, police gave Jed and an eerily silent Camille their blessing to leave. They'd taken both their cell numbers in the event they had further questions or needed them to serve as court witnesses.

Thankfully, no one was injured, but the teen gang members' paramedics said they'd suffered minor burns to their eyes.

They'd heal.

It was Camille's inner wounds Jed worried about.

Had this mess opened old scars she'd finally believed healed?

The whole ride home, the babies miraculously slept, but Camille didn't. She stared out the window, never saying a word.

Once he'd reached the turnoff to the ranch's dirt road, he said, "You're awfully quiet. Want to talk anything out?"

"No, thank you."

"You were a hero back there. If you hadn't intervened, there's no telling how many people may have been hurt."

He'd meant his words as a compliment, but she only seemed to shrink further inside herself.

At the house, it had already turned dark. He turned off the engine and said, "Let me handle the tenors. You go take a nice, long soak in the guest room tub. You've earned a little R & R."

"I know you mean well, but please stop coddling me."

"Babe, I'm not—"

"I'm fine." She unbuckled her seat belt, then left the car to sling the diaper bag with the bottles over her right shoulder. She next unfastened Allie's carrier from its base to take the infant into the house.

Jed grabbed Callie and Sallie, joining Camille in the

kitchen, where she was already cleaning out the diaper bag and prepping fresh bottles.

They fed the babies in silence.

Jed checked the animals, making sure they were settled for the night. He returned to the house to find the babies on their play mat and Camille still not talking.

They bathed the babies in more silence.

After tucking the girls in for the night, with still no words save for the briefest of pleasantries, he'd had enough.

"Please, Cam, let me in." In the hall with the nursery door closed, and monitor in hand, he said, "Given your aversion to violence, what went down in the store had to be a shock, but babe, it's over and—"

"What don't you get about the fact that it's never going to be over? I can't run far enough. I can't hide. I mean, look at you—your entire life is based on killing."

"Bullshit. My life is dedicated to protecting our country from terrorists who would love nothing more than to destroy our *peaceful* way of life."

"Great." She charged down the stairs. "That speech would make me feel so much better if you were ever to be blown to pieces by a suicide bomber."

He chased after her. "Where is this coming from? How did a couple of gangster teens transform you from the amazing woman I've come to know over the past few weeks into this angry shell?"

"Screw you, Jed." She turned for the front door. "If you don't care for my company, I've got an easy remedy."

"You're putting words in my mouth that I never said."

He tried pulling her into a hug. But she backed away, hugging herself.

"You don't understand." Her voice sounded raspy with what he could only guess was pain. "How it all came rushing back—the last case I worked. There was so much blood. Senseless, stupid killing. Five brothers and sisters just wiped out. Why? Because they were costing too much to feed, and the parents preferred to spend their government checks on meth. The children weren't even theirs, but foster kids. Society is broken beyond repair and…" She swiped tears from her cheeks.

"No," he said, "society is plugging along just like it always has, with some good apples and some bad. What sucks for you is that you spent years focused on the worst of the worst. Look what we've shared here— the beauty of our girls."

"They're not *our* girls, Jed."

"I know, but—"

"No, there's no gray area in this. Emily gave your mom custody. You're their uncle and I'm nothing to them."

"They adore you."

"That's too bad, because I'm leaving." She took her purse and keys from the entry hall table.

"No." He darted in front of her to block the door. "The girls need you. I need you. I—" He stopped short of telling her he loved her. Had always loved her. Because honestly, he wasn't even sure he knew what love was. When he'd married Alyssa, he'd meant his vows to her. He'd promised to spend a lifetime caring for her. But in hindsight, had what he'd shared with her been love? When she'd left, it hadn't squeezed his chest like a vise—not anywhere close to the physical agony this argument with Camille caused.

What did that mean?

Covering her face with her hands, she crumpled to the floor.

He sat cross-legged beside her, drawing her onto his lap, holding her, rocking her while she cried harder than any of his nieces on their worst day.

"What you went through is behind you," he said. "I know it's hard—trust me, I've seen things I'd rather forget, too. But with the help of the guys on my team, I've worked through it. Let me help you."

She nodded against his chest, clinging to him. "Take me to bed. I want to forget. I need to feel free."

Slipping his fingers beneath her chin, he coaxed her gaze to his. "You sure?"

She nodded, but then shook her head. "The only thing I'm sure of is wanting to be with you. Make love to me. Make me forget…"

Chapter 14

"Good morning, gorgeous…"

While Camille stood at the stove flipping pancakes, Jed pushed her hair aside, nuzzling her neck. They'd shared a beautiful night lost in each other's arms, but this morning she wasn't filled with just regret, but an avalanche of self-doubt. What had she been thinking? She'd had enough psychologist visits to know that masking her feelings with sex wasn't exactly the key to good mental health.

"Why didn't you ask me to help?" He nodded toward the girls, who were all grinning in their swings. "You did diaper changing and feeding by yourself?"

"It wasn't a big deal." She scooped two pancakes onto a platter. "You were sleeping, and since I was wide-awake, I figured at least one of us should be well rested."

A knock sounded on the back door.

Two seconds later, her grandfather waltzed in. "Good morning. Mmm…" He kissed her cheek. "Pancakes. My favorite."

Oblivious to the undercurrent running between Camille and Jed, Gramps helped himself to the booth. "If you don't mind, Earl would probably love a few pancakes, too. Oh, and I'd like a little sugar in my coffee today. Need extra pep in my step. I hit a promising vein yesterday that could finally be the motherlode."

"Good for you." Jed got her grandfather's coffee, setting it on the table in front of him.

"Thank you," Gramps said. "And you know, son, ever since you and my granddaughter patched things up, I think you'll make a fine addition to the family."

"We're not together." Camille set his pancakes in front of him a little harder than planned. She fared no better with the glass syrup bottle or his silverware and napkin.

"Mind heating that syrup?" Ollie asked. "I'll need butter, too."

"God bless America." She slapped the spatula to the counter. "You're demanding this morning."

"I've got it," Jed said. "You work on Earl's meal."

"It's not like you to be snippy." Gramps tucked his napkin into his shirt collar. "Lovers' quarrel?"

"Please, Gramps…" She clamped her hand over her forehead and sharply exhaled. "Just eat your breakfast and leave it alone."

"I'm trying to eat," he said, "but can't because I have no butter or warm syrup."

Camille gripped the counter hard enough for her knuckles to turn as white as the tile surface.

Sun shone through the many windows; the air smelled of a heavenly mix of pancakes and baby lotion and the leather of Jed's jacket, boots and cowboy hat. She should be happy. So why wasn't she? Why couldn't she forget the convenience store robbery and get on with her currently wonderful life?

Thirty minutes later, after three cups of heavily sugared coffee, Gramps and Earl finally moseyed to the mine. The mule had eaten six pancakes, leaving none for her.

Just as well.

It wasn't like she had much of an appetite.

"Hey…" Jed stood behind her at the sink. "Now that Ollie's gone, what gives?"

"I'm sorry."

"No need to apologize. Everyone has down days."

"It's not that. I'm apologizing for last night. It never should have happened."

"What do you mean?"

She turned in time to see his eyes narrow.

"Not to toot my own horn," he continued, "but you seemed awfully content after we…"

"It was a mistake. The sex was nothing more than putting a bandage over a gaping wound. This game I proposed of the two of us playing house was a horrible mistake. I'm not right in the head. Can't you see that?"

"What I see—" He reached for her, but she backed away. He hefted himself up to sit on the counter. "What I see is that until what happened in that convenience store, you and I have never been happier." He glanced at his hands, which he'd braced on his thighs. "Look, I wasn't planning on admitting this today, but it's going to come out eventually." His mother had gotten word to him that conditions were improving, and she'd be able to leave soon. "Being back with you feels like I finally found the missing piece to my life's puzzle. The thing is, I didn't even realize how incomplete I felt until this time with you and the girls. Mom should be home by next week, but as much as she loves her missionary work, what if I ask her to transfer primary custody of the tenors to me? *Us?* I'll need to finish out my current enlistment period, but what would it hurt for us to all live in Coronado for a while? Hell, if it makes you feel better, even Ollie and Earl could come along for the ride."

"Stop. What you're suggesting is ridiculous."

"No, Cam, it's brilliant. The best idea I've had in years. I hate that Chase and my sister died, but I'm not going to deny that I feel profoundly blessed that out of that tragedy you and I have somehow found each other. I think I love you, and I sure as hell love us being a couple again, don't you?"

"That's delusional. It's not me you love, but the idea of maintaining this cozy domestic bubble. But you know what the problem is with bubbles? They burst." Arms crossed, she paced. "Don't you get it? Up here, we're safe. The big, bad outside world can't touch us, but yesterday proved that the second we descend from this mountain, all hell's going to break loose."

"Now what's sounding delusional? You can't hide up here forever. I thought I could live with myself, just heading back to base and leaving the girls with my mom and you, but not only can't I saddle her with that, I don't want to."

"Good for you. I'm glad to see you stepping up to your responsibilities. In case you forgot, they don't involve me." The babies' swings were slowing, so she rewound them.

Giggles abounded.

"Know what I think?" he asked, hopping down from the counter.

"I don't care."

"Tough." He lightly grabbed her shoulders, forcing her to face him. "Does the idea of a life spent alone save for tending to Ollie and Earl sound appealing? Or would you rather face your demons like you did during that robbery? Throw coffee in the face of your every fear like the badass you were born to be. Don't you get it? You're a hero."

"No." After a sharp shake of her head, Camille said, "All I see is that my reckless actions resulted in spooking that teen into firing his gun. I was damn lucky any of us in that store survived. In hindsight, I should have tried disarming them. I didn't take time to think the whole thing through."

"You're not being rational. You did the only thing you could, and it worked. You're a rock star." He tried pulling her into a hug, but she brushed him away.

"I have to sort Ollie's meds and wash his sheets, and Lord only knows how many dishes have piled up."

"Please don't do this." He wasn't too proud to beg while trailing after her to the entry hall. "Don't go."

"I—I have to."

"When are you coming back?"

The look she cast toward the babies contained unmistakable love. "I'm not sure."

For at least five minutes, Jed stared at the closed front door, unsure what to do with his hands, or especially the wad of emotions balled in his stomach.

What. The. Hell.

How had he so drastically misread Camille's intentions? They'd been getting along better than they ever had. How could she not see that? How could she not crave more?

Lord, he'd love hashing this out with his buddies over a half-dozen cold brews, but whether Camille was here or not, his three tenors still needed care.

A glance out the front window showed that the once sunny day had turned cloudy. A northerly wind had also kicked up.

He took the stroller from the hall closet, bundled the girls to put them in it, then headed to the barn for morning chores.

"You'd better behave," he said to the chickens.

They eyed him as warily as he did them.

From outside the pen, the girls grinned at the fluffy fowl intent on pecking clear through the toe of Uncle Jed's boots.

The goats were adorable, surrounding him and the girls for sweet talk and petting.

"Should we go find Lucy and Ethel?" he asked his helpers.

They cooed and gurgled and made all the new weird and wonderful baby noises he'd learned to appreciate more every day.

The two horses had made it to the extreme far end of the pasture, where tender spring grasses formed a horse oasis.

"You two probably know Camille better than I do." He stroked their manes. "Wish you could tell me what to do. I'd never tell her, but she made a valid point..."

It's not me you love, but the idea of maintaining this

cozy domestic bubble. But you know what the problem is with bubbles? They burst.

Maybe he didn't love her?

Maybe his track record with relationships meant he didn't understand love? What he did understand and wholeheartedly believed in was the importance of family. And somehow, some way, Camille had once again become just that. An integral part of his family he wasn't sure he could let go.

Camille did laundry and dishes and dusted every flat surface in her grandfather's cabin. She found a roast in the freezer, defrosted it, then put it in the pressure cooker with carrots and onions and potatoes.

What she didn't do was think about Jed.

How he would manage caring for the animals with the babies in tow. She especially didn't worry about whether or not he'd dressed the girls warmly enough or remembered to screw the lids onto their bottles extra tight. Sallie had the beginnings of diaper rash. Would he remember to use her cream?

Stop.

This constant fretting about infants who weren't even hers wasn't healthy.

But they could be yours.

The intoxicating thought crept into her head like a wisp of smoke. Subtle. Not nearly enough to hurt her unless she took Jed up on his asinine offer. Neither of them were parent material, yet despite that fact, they'd managed to keep everyone reasonably content and thriving—even their pediatrician had said so at their well-child visit.

On the surface, following Jed and the triplets to

Coronado sounded like a great adventure. But what happened when the newness wore off? What happened when she was inevitably forced to face her demons again by encountering more crime? Or if, God forbid, Jed was hurt?

In a metropolitan area as big as southern California, there were bound to be multiple shootings weekly. How would she cope? What happened if she had the kids with her and had a meltdown? What if they were hurt? What if Jed shipped out to Syria or Iraq? What if she permanently lost him?

Worse, what if her neurotic fears caused him to no longer want her to be with him or around the babies? The sting of Jed's rejection might hurt too badly to ever recover.

All of which made staying on her grandfather's ranch the right choice. The only choice.

Without her to help care for his nieces, the most likely scenario was that Jed would return to the navy and Barbara would remain here to care for her granddaughters. Camille would happily help.

All problems solved.

All except for the one stemming from the fact that she'd fallen hard for Jed all over again.

The sound of a car crunching on the gravel drive had her looking out the window.

Jed.

And the three screaming tenors.

She smoothed her hair. Not wanting to see him, yet desperate to.

Knowing his pride would never have allowed him to come unless he needed her help, she raced out the door and across the porch, to find him already out of the car.

"What's wrong? Are they sick?"

"No clue." He swiped his hand through his too-long hair. "If I had to guess, I think they miss you."

"Not likely." She opened the SUV's back door, then unfastened Sallie's safety harness to lift her into her arms. "Poor baby. Is your tummy hurting?" When the infant calmed, she repeated the drill with the other two.

Remarkably, her voice, her hold, did seem to soothe them.

"What did I tell you?" Jed held Sallie and Callie while she still held Allie. "They missed you."

"I can't do this." Camille hated how her voice cracked. How very much she cared for all three of these babies and their uncle.

"Yes, you can. Come back to the house with me. We'll stay in separate rooms. But I need you. The girls need you."

"I can't. I was wrong to ever think we could keep this casual. I never should've stayed. As for you and me sleeping together? *Massive* mistake."

"You don't mean that."

"I do. I thought I could handle playing house with you. I thought once it came time for this to all end, I could handle that. Turns out…" she said on the heels of a broken sob "…I'm in even worse shape than I thought."

"What are you talking about?"

"You. Me. Us? We were always just a dream and you know as well as I do that dreams never come true."

"But what if they could?" After putting the babies in the car seats, he took her hands. "Have the past few weeks proved nothing? I don't know about you, but I've had a damned good time—the best of my life."

"You're only saying that because we've been play-acting at being a family. But we're not. Will never really be. As soon as your mom comes home, it will all be over, anyway. Why not rip off the proverbial bandage and end it now?"

"Why?" He pulled her against him for a fierce hug. "Because I don't want it to. *Never* want it to."

"Think about what you're saying. You're career military. I'm…" Escaping him, she flung up her free arm, only to slap it against her side. "I don't know what I am. I have no job. No ambition. No future."

"Knock it off. Of course you have a future—it's right here with us. You've had a career setback, but that doesn't mean your life is over or you'll never feel passion for your work."

She shook her head. "No. You're just saying that to make me feel better. The two of us as a couple would never work out. That's why we broke up a lifetime ago and you married another woman and—"

"Got a divorce and have only been with a handful of women since. And not because I felt anything for them, but because we satisfied mutual physical needs. With you, it's been different. Sex wasn't just sex, but it meant something—a fresh start for both of us."

"I—I want to believe you."

"Then do. You've been so quick to think the worst, but how about swinging the other way and focusing on a positive outcome?"

She wanted to believe him. She wanted to try being happy. She wanted to never again close her eyes and see the tragedy that had forever fundamentally changed her, but was that even possible?

"I'm afraid," she admitted.

"Of what?" He cradled her face with his hands.

"Everything." She leaned into his touch. "I'm afraid of falling for you and the girls, only to lose you all. I'm equally afraid of leaving you, only to live out my life alone."

He kissed her. Slowly and sweetly enough to ignite a yearning for more of him—*of them*—that flowed through her veins like sun-warmed honey.

"Say yes," he eventually said when they broke for air. "Yes to me and the girls and being happy."

"But how can I do that when the girls aren't even yours? What if your mom refuses to turn over custody?"

"Why would she do that? Now you're just making up excuses."

"They make perfect sense to me."

"That's the problem…" Releasing her, he backed away. "You're the only one who sees logic in your rationale. All I see is a woman so terrified by death that you're equally terrified by life."

Chapter 15

Back at the house, Jed loaded the tenors in their stroller, then did the evening chores.

The chickens pecked his ankles hard enough to damn near bust through his cowboy boots.

The goats were as sweet as usual, and Lucy and Ethel were patient enough to allow all three babies to stroke their manes.

By the time he finished, the girls were cranky.

He checked diapers to find two wet.

After a quick change, he was back downstairs making bottles and then feeding using Camille's assembly line method.

While making a sandwich for himself, he let them swing, then it was bath time and he put them to bed.

He took Emily's blanket from the crib, holding it to his face and dragging in the scent of her that by this time was probably a figment of his imagination. Putting it back in the crib, he carefully covered three pairs of feet and thirty tiny toes.

"I love you," he whispered in the dark room. "I'm not sure how it happened, but I love you more than I ever thought possible."

He cupped his hand to Sallie's head.

"I'm not sure how to work it out, but I want to be your dad. And I really want Camille to be your mom..."

Downstairs, the house phone rang.

"Sweet dreams, my little tenors." He gave the girls one last adoring look, then charged down the stairs to catch the phone.

He'd lost count of the number of rings before he grabbed the ancient phone's handset. "Hello?"

"Thank goodness," his mom said. "I was beginning to think you weren't home. I'm on a pay phone at Heathrow, so I'll make this quick. I fly out of here in an hour, land in Newark, then Denver, then Aspen. Mind picking me up?"

"Of course."

"Thank you." She gave him her flight number and arrival time. "I have to go, sweetheart. Are the babies okay?"

"We're all fine."

"Good. Sorry to rush. I haven't even begun to process..." A muffled sobbing sound made him wonder if she was crying. "I love you, hon. See you soon."

"Looking forward to it, Mom. Fly safe."

He hung up the phone and felt oddly empty. Hard to believe she was his last blood relative—well, aside from the girls, but he wouldn't be able to hold a decent conversation with them for a damned long time.

Since in the rush to answer the phone he'd forgotten the baby monitor, he returned to the nursery.

The girls had gravitated together, snuggling beneath their mother's blanket. A rush of love swept through him like a warm wave. He hadn't known himself capable of such deep emotion, but now that he knew, he never wanted to be without it.

He'd talk to his mom about what she wanted to do. But one way or another, he planned on playing a major role in his nieces' lives.

And Camille?

Where did she fit in?

He pressed his hands to his face, wishing his words had gotten through. Why couldn't she see herself like he did? She was amazing with the babies, always cooking and doing nice things for him and her grandfather. When was the last time she'd done something for herself?

He took the monitor and crept from the room, closing the door behind him.

The den was cold, but what was the point in making a fire just for himself?

Lonely, more than a little depressed, he grabbed a beer from the fridge, downed it in a few swigs, then went to bed, dreaming of Camille. Of the life they'd share if only she'd trust him enough to let him all the way in.

But then why would she?

The last time they'd been together, he'd chosen the navy over her. In asking her to return to California with him, wasn't he essentially doing the same thing all over again?

Chapter 16

"To what do I owe the pleasure of your company?" Gramps asked from his recliner. As usual, a Western blared on TV while he read a gold mining magazine.

"I missed you." Camille had curled onto the far end of the sofa, wrapped in one of her grandmother's well-loved quilts. She nursed a steaming mug of chamomile tea, wishing more than anything that she was snuggled next to Jed with the babies sleeping upstairs.

"Right. And John Wayne's stopping by in a bit for poker."

"Why wouldn't I miss you? We haven't had a real visit since I saw you at the mine."

"What are you talking about?" He paused his movie. "Me and Earl have been over to Chase and Emily's for a bunch of meals."

"I know, but those don't count. You mostly talked with Jed and I cooked and did dishes."

"Tired of domestic life?"

"What do you mean?" She fingered the quilt's rolled edge.

"I mean are you tired of being married with kids without having a ring on your finger?"

"Jed and I are just friends—barely even that."

"Lovers' quarrel?"

"Gramps!"

"What? I wasn't born yesterday. Any fool could see the sparks between you two. What's the problem?"

"The bigger question would be what isn't the problem? He pretty much asked me to marry him, then return to Coronado with him to help take care of the babies."

"And you don't think that sounds like a good idea?"

"Emily didn't leave him custody of his nieces, so there's that."

"If he wants to take on the role of their father, I can't imagine Barbara keeping him from them. Next problem?"

"Don't you have a movie to watch?" She picked up one of the mining magazines he'd left on the sofa and thumbed through it.

"I've seen this flick so many times I deliver most lines better than the actors."

"Show me. Sounds like fun to watch you act it out."

"Girl, what do I have to do to get you to realize there is no problem big enough to keep you from a man you love?" He slapped his journal to the side table next to his chair. "If this trouble with Jed has anything to do with your old job, you need to compartmentalize it. Shove it way in the back of your mind and get on with the business of living. What you faced in Miami can't define you. Running away won't make it better. Only truly living will tackle that job."

"Easier said than done."

"You think I didn't come home from the war with a few issues? The things I saw…" He whistled. "Those concentration camps were the worst sort of human atrocity. Entire generations of families killed for no better reason than a psycho ruler's whim. It was vile. Disgusting on a gut-deep level that literally gave me such disturbing nightmares I'd wake up dry heaving. Your grandmother would draw me a bath in that big ol' claw-foot tub, climb in behind me and hold me till I remembered that her and your mother were what was real. Everything else was in the past. Her advice didn't make what I'd seen any less awful, but eventually, the nightmares gave way to dreams of the sort of happy life I wanted for your mom."

"I'm sorry for what you went through. I really am, but—" Camille tossed the quilt off to stand in front of the window, arms folded, staring into the night. Facing him, she asked, "Did those dreams include my dad getting shot?"

"What happened to your father was a tragedy beyond words. Your grandmother and I weren't sure our Phoebe would make it through. But she did. And I like to think she enjoys her sunny Florida condo life." He took a butterscotch from the candy dish he kept next to the table's Tiffany-style lamp. After unwrapping it and popping it in his mouth, he said around it, "Another survivor? Jed's mom. She and his father shared a wonderful marriage. His death was incredibly hard on her, but look at her now. Traveling all over the globe, helping so many people. Jed's daddy would be proud."

"You make it sound like all these deaths worked out for the best. Chase and Emily's girls used to cry so hard from missing them that the only way I could console them was by covering them in the blanket from their parents' bed. And what about you? Are you happier with Grandma gone?"

"You know I'm not. I'll never forget what we shared, but she's gone and I'm still here. Sure, I could sit in this chair and mope all day every day, missing the past, but then I'd be throwing away my future." He snatched another candy from the bowl. "Do you think all those poor murdered children you mourn would begrudge your laughter with Jed and those baby girls? Don't you think Chase and Emily would rather see them raised with a mother and father?"

"Please stop." She literally couldn't take one more word. "You made your point. I'm glad you're thrilled with your lot in life, but I'm not."

Before he had the chance to share another story about how great everyone else was for handling their grief better than her, Camille dashed off to her room.

Maybe she'd eventually get over her ugly past, maybe she wouldn't. But the only way she'd find out was with time.

What if Jed doesn't want to wait?

What if just like the last time they'd broken up, he ran off and married his first rebound?

In her room, Camille shut and locked the door, flung herself across her bed and masked her sobs with her pillow.

Was she making a horrible mistake in not going to Jed and the babies this second? Or would opening herself up to them heart and soul, only to later lose them, prove emotionally catastrophic?

How would she ever know?

"You're so tan," Jed said to his mother at the Aspen airport, while waiting for her luggage. "You look good."

"Thanks." She winced, eyes shining with unshed tears. He knew her well enough to know she was barely holding it together. Losing her dignity in a public place wasn't an option. "Wish I felt the same inside."

His palms sweated on the stroller's handle while she knelt to kiss each of her granddaughters on the crowns of their downy heads. They'd been fussy in even the brief time Camille had been gone. Having suffered so much loss in their short lives, how much more could they be expected to take?

"It doesn't seem possible..." She stood, easing her oversize purse off her shoulder and digging through for a travel-sized pack of tissues. Plucking one out, she pressed it to the corners of her eyes. "I can't bear this." She pressed her hands to her chest. "I honest-to-God feel like I'm dying myself. How is this possible? I should have gone next—never Em. Last time I flew in, she was here, greeting me with her b-beautiful smile and a wildflower bouquet."

"Mom..." Jed was horrible at shit like this—and it was shit. Chase dying. His sister. His mother seconds from falling apart. Worse yet, he needed Camille to help navigate this river of grief, but she was gone, too.

It was all too much. But as the man of the family, he had no choice but to buck up, somehow get his mother to the car without a breakdown, then carry on.

At the moment, he hated Camille for leaving him

hanging when he'd never needed her more. But that wasn't entirely true, because he feared the real engine driving his turbulent thoughts was love for her.

For the amazing couple they might have been.

"I can't thank you enough for helping Jed with the girls."

"I'm glad I was here." Camille hugged Barbara, who had always been like her second mom.

The day was beyond glorious. Temperatures in the high seventies. Sky fathomless blue. Air ripe with the scents of ponderosa pine and wildflowers and new spring grasses.

Barbara had walked the mile trek to Ollie's cabin.

The girls grinned in their stroller, holding out their arms to Camille, breaking her heart all over again from the full force of her love for these tiny perfect creatures who could never be hers.

Where's Jed? Camille wanted to ask, but pride wouldn't allow her to.

"Is your grandfather here?" Barbara looked past Camille to the house.

"He and Earl left for the mine just before sunrise. Gramps is convinced he's found the motherlode."

Barbara laughed. "He's been finding it for the past forty years."

"At least he has something to get him out of bed in the morning." Camille unbuckled Sallie's safety harness, lifting her from the stroller and into her arms. Her slight weight felt indescribably good. Like holding a physical manifestation of contentment. "Mmm… I missed you."

"Mind if we talk?" Barbara sat on the porch steps.

She wore a wide-brimmed straw hat that she adjusted to shade her eyes from the bright midday sun.

"I thought we are talking?"

Jed's mom patted the space beside her. "I mean we need to really talk. If there's anything losing Em and Chase taught me, it's that life is too short and unpredictable to let a second go by without saying what needs to be said."

True. Hadn't Camille once used that very line of reasoning on Jed?

Holding Sallie on her lap, Camille settled on the step, but wasn't at all sure she cared to hear what Jed's mom had to say.

"I spent the morning making plans for Emily's memorial service. Call after call for flowers and a caterer. Musicians. Jed and I are holding it in that sweet little stone chapel at the top of Mount Celeste. The drive is a nightmare with all those twists and turns, but worth it for the view. Emily and Chase loved it up there. Emily scattered Chase's ashes to the wind from the mountain's peak, and I thought it only fitting that she join him."

"Sounds lovely," Camille said. Only she was lying, because nothing could be further from the truth. There wasn't one good thing about scattering the ashes of two beautiful souls who'd been far too young to die.

"I think so, too," she said in a resigned tone.

"Is there anything I can do to help?"

"As a matter of fact…" Barbara sucked in a swift breath, only to slowly release it.

Camille rested her pinkie against Sallie's palm.

The infant gave it a squeeze.

"Jed told me about the will. I'm not sure what Emily was thinking, leaving these amazing little creatures to

me, but I do know I'm too old to be a mom to triplets.
Jed and I have an appointment for next week with Baxter to arrange for me to start the paperwork necessary
for naming Jed the girls' legal guardian."

"What?" Camille's pulse raced. If he took the babies
to California, she might never see them again. Oh, he'd
bring them to the ranch for the occasional visit, but that
wasn't enough. If they stayed here with their grandmother raising them, then Camille could help.

"I know you love him."

"E-excuse me?" Camille shrank inside herself. Barbara had never been one to beat around the bush, but
this sort of declaration was too much even for her.

"Don't pretend you don't know what I'm talking
about. Everyone from your grandparents to your mother
to Jed's father and myself could always see you two
were meant to be together—just like Emily and Chase. I
can tell by the girls' reaction from just visiting that they
adore you. I also see your hand in all the little touches
around the house. Wild crocus on the kitchen sink windowsill. Homemade oatmeal cookies in the counter jar
and banana bread wrapped in foil. My granddaughters'
clothes folded just so and smelling fresh. My son moping as if he's lost not only his sister and brother-in-law,
but his best friend." She took Sallie's free hand for a
jiggle. "It's none of my business, but what happened
between you? Why aren't you with him now?"

"It—it's complicated." More complex than a single
conversation could ever convey.

"Figure it out."

"Barbara… You know how much I love and respect
you, but what did or didn't happen between your son
and me is a private, deeply personal matter."

"Not when he's hurting. Not when my granddaughters are losing a potential mother all over again."

Camille stood, crossing the short distance to tuck Sallie back into her stroller.

"How can you ignore his pain?" Barbara asked. "You have one of the biggest hearts of anyone I've ever known."

His pain? What about mine? Camille's hands shook as she fastened Sallie's harness. She kissed Allie and Callie on the crowns of their heads.

"Please, Camille. Talk to him. I know whatever happened between you can be worked out. You two deserve to finally have your happy ending."

"I don't mean to be rude," Camille somehow managed to say without bursting into tears, "but I have a lot to do. It would be best if you'd leave."

"If that's what you want." Confusion and hurt flashed across Barbara's dear, familiar features. "Emily's service will be held Saturday at two o'clock. I took the liberty of inviting your mom. We had a good chat, reminiscing about happier times. Jed took me to get a new phone. She texted me this morning that she'll be in on Friday. I figured she would've let you know by now?"

"She's big on surprises." And this was a doozy.

Nobody would be able to see through Camille's show of bravado faster than her mom. But that was okay. The two of them would have a nice visit, attend Emily's service, share a good cry, and then her mom would go back to her busy condo lifestyle and Camille would stay here with her grandfather and Earl.

It wasn't the dream life she'd so recently imagined, but it would do.

It had to.

Because she was fresh out of any other options.

* * *

Jed struggled to contain his disappointment in Camille—not just for leaving him, but the girls.

Since Camille's mother, Phoebe, had flown in that afternoon, Jed's mom had invited the whole Hall family for Friday night supper. Were it not for the reason behind this reunion—Emily's death and upcoming memorial service—this might have been a happy occasion.

With the girls content in their swings, Jed turned his attention to Camille, watching her chop tomatoes for the salad that would accompany his mom's famous lasagna—only he had no appetite.

Ollie had Phoebe cornered in the kitchen booth, regaling her with what he deemed irrefutable evidence of the motherlode he'd discovered in his mine.

How different the house had felt with Jed and Camille on their own. Like it belonged to them. Now, even though he was the legal owner, it didn't feel like his house, or Emily and Chase's, but his mom's.

Unable to maintain this charade of everything being normal between him and Camille a second longer, he set his Coors on the counter, then left his post in front of the toaster oven to whisper in her ear, "Come with me."

"Where?"

Ignoring her question, he took her hand. Also ignoring both their mothers' hopeful glances, he led her out the back door, across the yard and toward the barn.

"Slow down," Camille said. "Where are we even going?"

"Away." He opened the pasture gate.

Lucy and Ethel glanced up and whinnied.

With the sun just setting, the air still held the heat

of the day. A light fog rose from the field. The sky was awash in purples and orange.

"Your mom needs my help."

"News flash—my mom is a one-woman army. She handles the care of entire villages. I doubt putting the finishing touches on our meal will break her."

"If your plan was to drag me far enough from the house so we could argue in private, mission accomplished."

He released her hand and sighed, raking his fingers through his hair. "The last thing I want is to fight with you."

"Then what do you want?" Was it his imagination, or had her voice caught in her throat?

I don't know.

He'd wanted to be alone with her. To try explaining how miserable he'd been without her. But now? He didn't see a woman who had been longing for him standing before him, but a woman who'd determined she'd be better off without him or his nieces and was at peace with her decision.

"Look," he said, "I needed to touch base with you about tomorrow. I didn't want there to be awkwardness between us at Emily's service."

"Why would there be? Your sister was one of my oldest friends. I would never do anything to disrespect her or her memory. For you to think I would—" Lips clamped shut, she crossed her arms. "I should get back inside. Your mother needs me."

What's wrong with you that you can't see I need you?

She jogged across the field toward the house.

He strode toward the horses.

Reaching them, stroking their coarse manes, he said,

"You know your life is FUBAR when the woman you finally realize you love would rather chop tomatoes than spend one more second with you."

His confession earned a snort.

Chapter 17

"Everything okay?" her mother asked a few minutes after Camille slipped through the back door without Jed.

"Fine." She squared her shoulders and plastered on a smile. "Mmm… Dinner smells delicious."

Her mother's narrowed gaze told Camille her cheery act wasn't fooling anyone. "If there's anything you need to talk to me about, that's why I'm here. I can't imagine how tough it's been for you and Jed caring for the girls."

"It wasn't bad." *As strange as it may seem, I had the time of my life, playing house with the man I thought I loved.* But that was before she'd realized that love was incapable of being sustained for any real length of time.

"What aren't you telling me?"

"Nothing." Camille forced another smile. Turning to Barbara, she asked, "Want me to set the table?"

"That would be great," Jed's mother said. "I forget you probably know where things are better than I do. It's been ages since I lived here, and Emily rearranged the whole place to her—" Tears welled in her gorgeous green eyes that were the exact shade of her son's. "Sometimes the pain of losing her feels more than I can bear."

"Come here…" Phoebe brushed past Camille to give her friend a hug. "Somehow, we'll get through this together."

"Thank you for coming. You're one of my oldest and dearest friends."

"Likewise."

Camille's throat ached at the sight of her mom and Barbara's heartfelt exchange.

She needed a hug, too, but she was on her own.

Nothing new.

But a fact she'd learn to get used to.

Saturday morning, Jed hugged his sister's urn, staring out at the panoramic view from atop Mount Celeste. The intimate stone chapel had been filled to capacity with mourners, and after the service they had all taken the short hike up the stairs leading to the cross at the mountain's peak.

The day couldn't have been more perfect with balmy temperatures, a light breeze and a clear blue sky that made it seem as if the whole world had been spread before them in a jagged patchwork quilt of peaks and valleys and diamond-strewn lakes.

"I miss you, sis…" Could Emily hear him? He hoped so.

In his peripheral vision he saw Camille with both their moms and the babies. She wore a black dress that

hugged her every curve and made him feel like a slime-
ball for noticing.

You're at your sister's funeral, for Christ's sake.
Keep your shit together.

For an instant, their gazes locked, but she looked
away.

Her issues were bigger than anything he could handle. He would soon legally be a father and his responsibility to his nieces trumped all.

His mother moved to the base of a twenty-foot
wooden cross that on a clear day like this could be
seen from as far away as downtown Aspen.

"If you all would please gather..." She waved her
hands, urging their friends closer. "First, on behalf of
myself and Jed and my granddaughters, I can't thank
all of you enough for being here to celebrate the life
of my baby girl. Of course, Emily was a fully grown
woman with a family all her own..." For an instant, she
closed her eyes while swallowing hard. "For me, I will
always see her the day she was placed into my arms—
a red-faced, squirmy bundle who seemed more than a
little miffed that her cozy world had been upturned."
She laughed through silent tears. "I adored her at first
sight, as did her daddy and big brother."

Up until now, Jed had managed to keep his cool,
but the mental image of the first time he'd seen Emily
seemed as fresh in his mind as the scene unfolding before him. Five years older than the tiny creature, he
hadn't been sure what Emily's arrival meant for their
family, but to see how happy the baby made his folks...
Well, he'd decided to be happy, too. And love her. And
watch over her.

So how could he have let her die on his watch?

Tears stung his eyes, but for his mother, he had to stay strong.

"Our Emily may have earned a fancy economics degree, but all she ever really wanted was to be a wife and mother. When she and Chase first learned she was carrying triplets, instead of being terrified at the thought of never sleeping—" All present laughed at the welcome humor "—she was over-the-moon happy, devouring every baby care book she could. She and Chase loved each other for as long as I can remember. Losing him was a burden she simply wasn't able to bear. But that's okay. Jed and I will ensure her girls never forget just how amazing their mom and dad truly were. I hope as they grow and become contributing members of this community she also loved, that all of you will share your memories of her and their father with them. I'm a firm believer in remembering happy times and letting go of the bad." She dabbed a tissue to her eyes. "In that spirit, please join me in silent prayer while Jed releases her soul to be free with her husband's…"

A lumberjack of a kilt-wearing bagpipe player stepped up beside his mother, and while he performed the haunting strains of "Amazing Grace," Jed removed the urn's lid and offered his sister's ashes to the wind.

Eyes stinging, throat on fire from holding back tears, he found the task the hardest he'd ever done.

More than anything, he longed for Camille to be alongside him with her arm around his waist, letting him know she cared.

He knew with every bone in his body that she very much cared. The problem was figuring out how to break through her fears to allow room in her heart for hope.

With the urn emptied, he set it at the base of the cross.

His proud mother stoically held back tears, listening to the somber song, staring out at the vast blue where her beloved daughter now resided among angels.

Steeling his jaw, Jed looked to the crowd to find Camille silently sobbing. She held a tissue over her nose and her shoulders bobbed with each racking onslaught of silent tears.

His mother must have also seen her, as she placed her hand on his arm, whispering for only him to hear, "Go to her. She needs you more than I do."

"Sure?"

"Absolutely. Tell her how much you love her. And that you're never going to let her go."

He looked from her to Camille, who had discreetly backed away from those gathered to run down the stairs toward the parking lot, and he knew his mother was right.

He would go after his love, his best friend, the woman who would hopefully be the mother to his new daughters. He would ask her to marry him and he wouldn't take no for an answer...

Free from her fellow mourners, Camille ran until her lungs burned in the thin mountain air.

She wasn't sure what had happened. Maybe it was the somberness of the bagpipes playing the world's most depressingly beautiful song? Or Barbara's heartbreaking words? Or remembering playing Barbies with Emily when they'd been girls and chasing boys with her once they'd grown older?

Tears flowed so fast and hard she could barely find her car, and then her images of Emily melded into the grisly crime scenes that were the driving force behind her withdrawal from the world.

The pain was too much.

Crushing her from all directions.

But then Jed was beside her, embracing her with his tree trunk arms. So strong and solid and everything she'd ever needed and wanted and more.

"Shh…" He rocked her, rubbing his hand up and down her back. "It's okay. Everything's going to be okay."

"B-but it's not. I miss Chase and your sister. My dad and grandma. And I can't stop thinking of the victims from my cases—dozens of them. So many were just babies—like your girls—helpless and innocent and sweet, but monsters took them and I'm so afraid of those same monsters returning for me and you and the girls and never letting any of us go." The pain—*the raw terror*—crushed her from the inside out. Would any amount of comfort ever bring her peace? "Why does so much more bad happen than good?"

"It might seem that way, but it's not true. Yes, what happened to Emily and Chase and your father and all those children you mourn is awful, but that doesn't give you the right to give up." He held her even closer, as if hoping to convey through his physical strength how much he believed in his healing words. "Bad shit is always going to happen, but you have to rise above. When you and I ended things the first time, when Alyssa cheated on me, I never thought love was for me. But lo and behold, through unspeakable tragedy, I found you all over again." He framed her face with his hands. "Cam, I don't know how it happened, but I need you. I love you. Marry me? Be the forever mom my nieces already adore."

Yes! Camille's heart cried, but her more rational brain refused.

"You don't love me," she said, stepping back. "You love the idea of a live-in nanny for all those babies. I'm a wreck. You don't want to be anywhere near me."

"Seriously? I pour out my heart to you and that's all you can say?" He raised his hands in surrender. "You're going to stand there accusing me of wanting nothing more than to marry you only to use you?" He shook his head. "I want you to be happy, Camille. Maybe that won't be with me, but if getting there means seeking counseling for what happened in Miami, you need to do it."

Just as abruptly as he'd appeared, Jed left.

The pain of watching him walk away hurt worse than anything she'd ever been through—even all the trauma she'd witnessed in Miami.

Should she chase after him? Beg him for a second chance? Apologize for letting her fears spill out, over-riding the truth spoken by her heart?

He was 1000 percent right. She did need professional help to get her head in the same place as her gut, which was screaming at her to find Jed and to never let him go.

Camille darted among the mourners descending from the mountain peak. She ran into old friends wanting to make small talk. Gramps asked when they'd get something to eat.

Through all of these trivial encounters, she bobbed and weaved through the crowd, desperate to find Jed and make things right. But sadly, he was nowhere to be found.

Finally, she at least found his mom. "Where's Jed? Have you seen him?"

"I thought he was with you. He needed the keys to my car—I rented a cute little compact in Aspen because the SUV is too much for me to drive. He asked if I could handle it just this once to take the babies home."

"He already left?" Camille's stomach fell with disappointment.

"I'm pretty sure. Since he's looking for you, maybe he's going to your grandfather's place to—"

"Could you please drive Ollie home? I've got to find Jed."

"Of course, honey." Barbara didn't try hiding her concern. "Is everything all right?"

"No…" She was already turning for her car. "But I hope once I find him, it soon will be."

Judging by her runaway pulse, Camille wished she felt as sure as she'd sounded.

Jed had to forgive her. He just had to.

And if he didn't?

Well, she'd revert back to Plan A. *He had to.* Because any chance of turning her life around meant Jed and the girls would be in it.

Fury didn't begin to describe the slow burn spreading through Jed's body. He wanted nothing more than to help Camille, but how could he do that when she refused to help herself?

He didn't doubt for a moment that her Miami caseload had left indelible scars, but he couldn't grasp the fact that she preferred being alone to seeking help. If not from him, then from a professional who dealt with this kind of job-related PTSD.

He had a lot of SEAL brothers who'd been almost taken down by the mental illness. It wasn't something to be ashamed of but to conquer, just like any of the other battles they'd fought.

The winding dirt road clinging to the mountain's edge was barely wide enough for two cars to pass. The drop-off was sheer and hundreds—if not thousands—of feet down.

Ask him if he cared.

The new father in him told him to slow the hell down, but the cocky SEAL spurred him ever faster. He had to get down from here—away from the woman making him feel as if he was losing his mind.

Hugging the side of the mountain, the road wound in ever-tighter hairpin turns. He switched on the stereo, activating the FM's auto-search feature until settling on Metallica. He might be a cowboy at heart, but sometimes a body needed loud bass.

The cliff side was steeper than ever, but the lower in elevation he traveled, the more pines grew in spotty patches.

The more he thought about Camille, the harder he pushed the car. She made him feel helpless—not a good state for a SEAL accustomed to winning. He'd poured out his heart to her and she'd stomped on it, right in the parking lot of the chapel where they'd just attended his sister's—

He rounded the next corner to encounter a herd of bighorn sheep in the road's center. Jed swerved to miss them, but given his speed and the road's narrow width, there was nowhere to go but over the edge...

Excited to start this new chapter of her life, emboldened by her decision to trust in Jed to never hurt her, and in both of them to protect the girls, Camille chased after him to not only apologize, but tell him she'd be honored to marry him—if he'd still have her.

As tricky as the narrow dirt road was to navigate, she was surprised she hadn't caught up with him. But then that was just as well, given that they'd both need to pull over for all she had to say.

She'd driven a good ten to fifteen minutes, lightly trembling from the plunging drop-off alongside the non-existent shoulder, when she saw a sight that made her blood run cold.

No.

Please, God, don't let me lose Jed, too. Not when I've only just found him again.

The tail end of his mother's compact rental car tee-tered on the edge of the cliff, the front end barely supported by a few scraggly pines.

Holding her breath, Camille swerved left, parking on the inside of the switchback curve, as close to the towering cliff as possible. With the engine off, she scrambled out the passenger-side door. *"Jed!"*

A horrible screeching sound stopped her heart.

Then the crack of one scrawny pine. And another and another, before a heaving metallic groan served as a pre-lude to the vehicle careening down the mountainside.

"No...! Jed!"

Losing him now would be unfathomably cruel.

"Jed!" she screamed. "Don't you dare leave me!" Crumpling onto the dirt road, she covered her face with her hands, sobbing at the injustice of her entire stupid life. "Please... I don't want you to go..."

"I'm not going anywhere..." said a faint voice from below her.

"Jed?" She scrambled to her feet and ran toward the

sound, to find him perched on a narrow ledge just below the road. "*Ohmygod.* You're alive."

Once he'd pulled himself up onto the roadside, she dropped to her knees and held him tightly.

"I love you. I love you," she said, pressing dozens of kisses on every inch of his precious face. "I've always loved you. I'm so sorry for letting my hang-ups come between us. You were right. I do need counseling about the things I've seen, but mostly I need you and the girls. I need us to be the family I know we can be." She kissed him again—this time on his lips. "I'm still afraid—of everything—but for once, with you, my hope for the future is bigger than the fear. If your offer is still good, I'd love nothing better than to be your wife for the next fifty years."

Still stunned from his near brush with death, he shook his head. "Woman…"

"You don't want to marry me?" Her heart plummeted further than his mother's rental car.

"Of course I do." He kissed her again. "But after all you've put me through, I'd rather aim for a bit longer. Make it sixty and we have a deal."

Epilogue

"*Cam!*" Jed had to look twice to believe what he was seeing.

After two years in Coronado, he'd been honorably discharged. They'd spent the weekend driving home to the ranch—him behind the wheel of a U-Haul and Camille with the girls in the SUV.

As the father of three toddlers, he was used to them causing major household upheaval, but this latest stunt signaled the start to a whole new era of three-tenors trouble.

He'd just unloaded their plastic toy kitchen into the corner of the den Camille had designated as a play area, then headed back outside for a load of boxes, when he noticed the darlings had escaped their kitchen playpen where he'd stashed them for Camille to watch while she unpacked.

"Jed?" she called from the office they would share for ranch business. His first fifty head of cattle would be delivered next Wednesday. He couldn't wait to turn his family land into a working ranch again. "Everything okay? Printer paper mixed in with the…" Entering the den, she stopped to slowly exhale. "Please tell me I'm not seeing what I'm seeing…"

The girls had outdone themselves.

In the year since they'd been walking, they'd made some hellacious messes, but this one beat them all.

While Sallie had had her way with Camille's makeup case, putting lipstick on not only her sisters, but the walls, carpet, furniture and his mother's favorite lamp, Callie must've visited the fridge.

A few dozen eggs from the chickens that still hated him had been smashed into the pretend fry pan that had come with the pretend kitchen.

Meanwhile, Allie had gotten her hands on a few cans of soda. She entertained herself by shaking them as hard as she could, then wildly giggling when she opened them, only to watch them explode, raining sticky cola all over the already disgusting mess.

"Please tell me this is a nightmare," Camille said. "I literally left them alone in the kitchen for under a minute. How did this happen?"

"Babe…" He rested his arm across her shoulders. "I seriously wish you were sleeping, because that would mean I don't have to get out the carpet cleaner right after unloading the truck."

"Are we going to survive till their eighteenth birthdays?"

Allie opened another can, showering them all with

fresh cola. Her sisters danced and shrieked and clapped in the soda rain.

"In the immortal words of the Magic 8-Ball you said they were too young to have—*outlook doubtful.*"

Camille groaned. "When is the grandparent brigade descending?"

"I thought Tuesday, but I forgot to tell you that they're ahead of schedule and should be here fairly early tomorrow."

"Swell." Since she and Jed married, love must've been in the air, as Barbara married Dr. Daniel, whom she'd worked with for years in Africa. Camille's mother had married a retired stock analyst she'd met at a condo casino night, and had since moved to Boca Raton. Both couples had rented an RV and opted for a good old-fashioned road trip to come see the girls.

"Knock, knock…" Ollie strolled through the open front door. "What happened? I've looked after the place and all your animals for two years and this is the thanks I get?"

Earl trailed after him up the front porch stairs.

"Gaapaa!" The girls knew and loved him from his visits to Coronado and frequent video calls. Abandoning the scene of their multiple crimes, they attacked him with sticky hugs.

"There're my favorite girls—a little young for makeup, Miss Sallie, but it's a good look on you." He swooped her, shrieking, into his arms. "You're clearly destined for modeling."

"Me…!" Callie held up her arms, pinching her fingers. *"Me, Gaapaa!"*

Allie joined her sister in demanding to be lifted.

Ollie started to heft the other two girls, but Jed

stopped him by plucking up the two sticky rug rats himself. "Don't throw out your back."

"How about helping me get everyone in the tub?"

"Yessir." Both men were aimed for the stairs when a clacking on the entry hall's wood floor had them turning in that direction.

Hee-haw, hee-haw… Earl had strolled inside and now munched the side table's dried flower arrangement.

"I give up." Camille groaned, then covered her face and laughed. "We might as well let the whole crew inside. Lord knows this house can't get any messier."

"Lucy and Ethel are welcome. The goats, too." Jed said. "But those devil chickens? No way."

"Oh—" Ollie froze at the foot of the stairs. "Something I've been meaning to tell both of you—well, aside from me finally hitting the motherlode, but that can wait."

"What's more important than that, Gramps?"

He looked to each of them in turn. "Told you so."

"Huh?" Camille cocked her head.

Ollie busted out laughing. "I always said you two would end up together, and from the looks of it, this marriage is a lifelong deal. Lordy, how I love being right."

* * * * *

SPECIAL EXCERPT FROM

HARLEQUIN®

SPECIAL EDITION

*Alyssa Santangelo has no memory of the
past seven years—including her divorce—but she
remembers her love for Connor Bravo. One way
or another, she's going to get her husband back.*

Read on for a sneak preview of
A Husband She Couldn't Forget,
*the next book in Christine Rimmer's
The Bravos of Valentine Bay miniseries.*

An accident. I've been in an accident. The stitches they'd
put in her knee throbbed dully, her cheeks and forehead
burned and she had a mild headache. Every time she took
a breath, she remembered that the seat belt had not been
very nice to her.

She must have made a noise, because as she sagged
back to the pillow again, Dante flinched and opened
his eyes. "Hey, little sis." He'd always called her that,
even though she was second eldest, after him. "How you
feelin'?"

"Everything aches," she grumbled. "But I'll live."
Longing flooded her for the comfort of her husband's
strong arms. She needed him near. He would soothe all
her pains and ease her weird, formless fears. "Where's
Connor gotten off to?"

Dante's mouth fell half-open, as though in bafflement at her question. "Connor?"

He looked so befuddled, she couldn't help chuckling a little, even though laughing made her chest and ribs hurt. "Yeah. Connor. You know, that guy I married nine years ago—my husband, your brother-in-law?"

Dante sat up. He also continued to gape at her like she was a few screwdrivers short of a full tool kit. "Uh, what's going on? You think you're funny?"

"Funny? Because I want my husband?" She bounced back up to a sitting position. "What exactly is happening here? I mean it, Dante. Be straight with me. Where's Connor?"

Looking for more satisfying love stories
with community and family at their core?

Check out **Harlequin® Special Edition**
and **Love Inspired®** books!

New books available every month!

CONNECT WITH US AT:

Facebook.com/groups/HarlequinConnection

 Facebook.com/HarlequinBooks

Twitter.com/HarlequinBooks

Instagram.com/HarlequinBooks

Pinterest.com/HarlequinBooks

ReaderService.com

**ROMANCE WHEN
YOU NEED IT**

HFGENRE2018

Looking for inspiration in tales
of hope, faith and heartfelt romance?

Check out **Love Inspired®** and
Love Inspired® Suspense books!

New books available every month!

CONNECT WITH US AT:

Facebook.com/groups/HarlequinConnection

 Facebook.com/HarlequinBooks

 Twitter.com/HarlequinBooks

 Instagram.com/HarlequinBooks

 Pinterest.com/HarlequinBooks

ReaderService.com

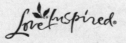

LIGENRE2018R2

*Could a pretend Christmastime courtship
lead to a forever match?*

Read on for a sneak preview of
Her Amish Holiday Suitor, *part of Carrie Lighte's
Amish Country Courtships miniseries.*

Nick took his seat next to her and picked up the reins, but before moving onward, he said, "I don't understand it, Lucy. Why is my caring about you such an awful thing?" His voice was quivering and Lucy felt a pang of guilt. She knew she was overreacting. Rather, she was reacting to a heartache that had plagued her for years, not one Nick had caused that evening.

"I don't expect you to understand," she said, wiping her rough woolen mitten across her cheeks.

"But I want to. Can't you explain it to me?"

Nick's voice was so forlorn Lucy let her defenses drop. "I've always been treated like this, my entire life. *Lucy's too weak, too fragile, too small, she can't go outside or run around or have any fun because she'll get sick. She'll stop breathing. She'll wind up in the hospital.* My whole life, Nick. And then the one little taste of utter abandon I ever experienced—charging through the dark with a frosty wind whisking against my face, feeling totally invigorated and alive... You want to take that away from me, too."

She was crying so hard her words were barely intelligible, but Nick didn't interrupt or attempt to quiet her. When she finally settled down and could speak normally again, she sniffed and asked, "May I use your handkerchief, please?"

"Sorry, I don't have one," Nick said. "But here, you can use my scarf. I don't mind."

The offer to use Nick's scarf to dry her eyes and blow her nose was so ridiculous and sweet all at once it caused Lucy to chuckle. "*Neh*, that's okay," she said, removing her mittens to dab her eyes with her bare fingers.

"I really am sorry," he repeated.

Lucy was embarrassed. "That's all right. I've stopped blubbering. I don't need a handkerchief after all."

"*Neh*, I mean I'm sorry I treated you in a way that made you feel…the way you feel. I didn't mean to. I was concerned. I care about you and I wouldn't want anything to happen to you. I especially wouldn't want to play a role in hurting you."

Lucy was overwhelmed by his words. No man had ever said anything like that to her before, even in friendship. "It's not your fault," she said. "And I do appreciate that you care. But I'm not as fragile as you think I am."

"Fragile? You? I don't think you're fragile at all, even if you are prone to pneumonia." Nick scoffed. "I think you're one of the most resilient women I've ever known."

Lucy was overwhelmed again. If this kept up, she was going to fall hard for Nick Burkholder. Maybe she already had.

Don't miss
Her Amish Holiday Suitor *by Carrie Lighte,*
available October 2019 wherever
Love Inspired® books and ebooks are sold.

Love Harlequin romance?

DISCOVER.

Be the first to find out about promotions, news and exclusive content!

f Facebook.com/HarlequinBooks

🐦 Twitter.com/HarlequinBooks

Instagram.com/HarlequinBooks

p Pinterest.com/HarlequinBooks

ReaderService.com

EXPLORE.

Sign up for the Harlequin e-newsletter and download a free book from any series at **TryHarlequin.com.**

CONNECT.

Join our Harlequin community to share your thoughts and connect with other romance readers! **Facebook.com/groups/HarlequinConnection**

ROMANCE WHEN YOU NEED IT

HSOCIAL2018